D1060002

Praise For Maynard Sims

"*Stillwater* is a great ghost story. The atmosphere is haunting from the start, and tension increases with every page. This is an atmospheric, creepy story and ideal for fans of ghost stories."

—I Heart Reading

"Maynard Sims succeeds in terrifying where some other more graphic authors fail."

—Masters of Terror

"A voice both uniquely entertaining and profoundly disturbing."

—Brian Keene, author of *The Rising*

"One word describes this novel to a T: wow. A non-stop roller coaster ride of pure horror from beginning to end."

—Night Owl Reviews on *Nightmare City*

"Sims inspires terror with killings that blend raw animal savagery and an intelligent sense of planning."

—*Publishers Weekly* on *Stronghold*

Look for these titles by Maynard Sims

Now Available

Nightmare City
Stronghold
Stillwater

The Department 18 Series
The Eighth Witch
A Plague of Echoes

Mother of Demons

Maynard Sims

SAMHAIN PUBLISHING

Samhain Publishing, Ltd.
11821 Mason Montgomery Road, 4B
Cincinnati, OH 45249
www.samhainpublishing.com

Mother of Demons
Copyright © 2015 by Maynard Sims
Print ISBN: 978-1-61922-982-2
Digital ISBN: 978-1-61922-749-1

Editing by Don D'Auria
Cover by Kelly Martin

First Samhain Publishing, Ltd. electronic publication: August 2015
First Samhain Publishing, Ltd. print publication: August 2015

Dedication

For our mothers, Dorothy and Rose—neither of them demons.

Chapter One

High above street level in Clerkenwell, she climbed up to the balcony's railing and rested her naked foot on the ice-cold metal. A brisk wind was coming in from the east, gusting across the balcony and raising goose bumps on the girl's pasty-white skin. From inside the penthouse, the four boys watched her climb.

"Go, girl," one of the boys—Finbar Clusky—called out. The other three laughed.

"Where's Erik?' another of them—Terry Butler—said. "Shouldn't he be here? This is for his benefit, isn't it? Hey, Alice. Don't jump…not yet. Your main audience isn't here yet."

The girl glanced back into the room. "I'm not going to jump, silly. I'm going to fly. I'm going to soar, above the clouds, to the heavens. There I will take my rightful place with the other goddesses."

"Is that what you are, Alice, a goddess?" Davy Coltrane said.

"I am Artemis, goddess of the moon, goddess of the hunt. And once I've taken my rightful place in the heavens, I will hunt you all down and make you kneel before me."

"Not Artemis, my love, but *Hecate*, the goddess of sorcery and magic."

All eyes turned to stare at the speaker: a man, older than any of them, handsome, with a chiseled Mediterranean face and piercing coal-black eyes. They all shrank back in their seats and cast their gazes to the floor. All except the girl who, from her perch on the balcony, looked at the man, her eyes clouded with confusion. "But, Erik, you're here. I thought you had gone away."

"I'm here, my love. I would never leave you."

"Erik, I can fly. I want to show you."

He smiled at her indulgently. "I know," he said. "I know you can fly. You can soar, as high as a bird, more graceful than an eagle. You don't have to prove it to me. One day we will fly together."

She looked uncertain. "Do you promise?"

"On my life." Erik Strasser bent low and whispered in Clusky's ear, "How much did you give her?"

"The usual amount. Nothing excessive."

"But now she believes she's a bird," Strasser said.

"No, a goddess," Mikey Gibson said, trying to lighten an atmosphere that had suddenly turn to stone.

Strasser silenced him with a look and turned again to the girl. "Come in now, my darling. Come in and get warm. Your skin is turning blue."

Alice looked at him questioningly for a moment, then down at her naked body. She shrugged, stepped down from the balcony and took a step inside the penthouse. Strasser reached forward and wrapped his arms around her shivering body. Gently he led her through to the bedroom and laid her down on the bed, covered her with a quilt, waited until her shivering had stopped and then watched a tear trickle down her cheek.

"Erik, I want to go home," she said, in a voice so small that he had to lean forward to hear what she was saying.

"And so you will. Tomorrow you can go back and see your mother, just as we discussed."

"Promise?"

"Of course. I give you my word." He reached out and stroked her forehead, smoothing her long blonde hair away from her brow.

"Thank you, Erik. You're so kind to me."

Her eyes fluttered shut, and within a moment her breathing had deepened and she was asleep.

He stared down at her, a frown creasing his forehead, and then he stepped away from the bed and went back into the lounge.

"Who was responsible for that?" he demanded, his accent thickening as his anger increased.

"Just a bit of fun," Butler said.

"No harm in it." That from Coltrane.

"And that's what you would have told the police once they'd scooped her body up off the pavement?"

"They didn't mean anything by it, Erik," Clusky said. "You're overreacting."

Strasser spun around to face him, his brow furrowed, his eyes blacker than ever.

Clusky grabbed his midriff and bent double as an icy hand gripped his intestines and started to twist. "Please," he gasped. "Don't."

"Don't blame Fin. It wasn't his fault," Coltrane said.

"Then whose fault was it? I left Finbar in charge."

"I was only having a laugh," Coltrane continued. "I didn't think the silly bitch would react so badly. I only gave her another shard. How was I to know she would go all goddess on us?"

Strasser turned on him. The skin of his brow had smoothed out, but the eyes burned just as deeply. "Get out," he said in little more than a whisper. "Get out of here and don't come back."

The boy stood up to his full height and thrust out his chin to show he wasn't going to be intimidated by Strasser. "Suit yourself. I'm going. This was a lousy gig anyway." He turned to Clusky, who was slowly straightening up, the color gradually returning to his face. "I don't go much on your choice of friends, Fin. Especially this wanker."

Clusky gave a small, almost imperceptible shake of his head, but Coltrane, nostrils flaring in anger, ignored it. "I'm outa here," he said, stalked to the door and yanked it open, slamming it shut behind him.

"Indeed you are," Strasser said softly.

Minutes later Davy Coltrane was on the platform of Farringdon Underground

Station, listening to the steady rumble of the approaching train.

The train's headlamps pierced the gloom as it appeared from around a bend in the track. As the train pulled into the station, Coltrane took a step forward… and then another.

The train hit him before he could fall from the edge of the platform. It carried his body along for a few yards until it slipped down the cold metal and disappeared under the grinding wheels.

Chapter Two

Jason West pushed open the door to the library and stepped into the cavernous book-lined room.

Violet Bulmer sat in the corner, the desk lamp catching the gray flecks in her copper hair. She looked sixty but he knew her age to be thirty-nine. The last few years had not been kind to her.

"Hello, Vi."

She looked up, peering at him over her half-rimmed glasses, and pushed a stray lock of her wild hair away from her face. "I didn't expect you to show," she said. "Not after the last time."

"You called, I came. That was the deal."

"I wouldn't have blamed you…"

"How long were you in hospital?" he said.

"Three weeks. You?"

"Six. I was pretty beaten up. What have you got?"

There was an empty seat beside her. She patted the cushion. "Come and see."

He sat down next to her at the desk and stared down at the file she had open in front of her. He picked up an eight-by-ten, black-and-white photograph of a smartly dressed young man exiting a famous eatery in Piccadilly.

"Who is he?"

"Erik Strasser, former CEO of Hematite Software and high priest of one of the fastest growing covens in the country."

"Why haven't I heard of him?"

"Up until a year ago he was based at Hematite's head office in Dusseldorf, and then, for reasons that were never made clear, he was relieved of his post. So he upped sticks, relocated to London and continued to spread his vile philosophy here in our backyard."

"Where's he living?"

"He has a penthouse apartment in Clerkenwell and a country pile in the Cotswolds."

"And the coven?"

"He also owns a converted warehouse in Docklands. As far as I understand it, they hold regular meetings there."

He dropped the photograph back onto the desk. "And your interest is? Apart from the obvious."

She drew in a deep breath and let it out through pursed lips. "Strasser is pure evil. The reason his coven has grown so rapidly is because he targets young people, mid to late teens, early twenties—vulnerable people disaffected by modern society and the teachings of the church."

"I would have said that accounts for the majority of the youth of today."

Violet gave him a withering look. "Cynic."

"Just an observation."

She shook her head. "I suppose I can't expect you to change, Jason."

He smiled. "How long have you known me?"

"Too long," she said, allowing her own smile to flit across her lips. "Strasser's like a disease, spreading his poison and infecting anyone who crosses his path."

He listened to the vitriol in her words. "This is personal," he said. "Isn't it?"

Violet looked at him long and hard, as if assessing whether or not to tell him. Finally, she looked away and stared down at the file. "I have a niece, Alice, my sister's girl. Bright, pretty little thing…at least, she was."

"And now?"

"I barely recognize her. My sister has her in a clinic in Hampshire."

"What happened to her?"

"Strasser happened to her. She met him during her final year at Oxford. She thought the lifestyle Strasser was offering would be fun and exciting. Within three months, Alice was heavily addicted to methamphetamine and was very quickly going downhill."

"How did your sister get her away from him?"

"The silly girl came home, to touch Stephanie for money. Said she needed it to further her studies. My sister may be many things, Jason, but she's not a fool. She could see from Alice's appearance that something was badly wrong. She promised to help Alice financially, and insisted she stay the night, with the promise that the next day they'd go to the bank together and make a withdrawal for the amount Alice was looking for. Instead she locked Alice in her bedroom and sought help from a friend of hers, a doctor with a private practice. Of course he was risking his career by helping her, but Stephanie can be very persuasive. Alice was committed to the clinic a few days later."

"And Strasser?"

"He came looking for Alice. He turned up at the house, as bold as brass, and demanded that my sister release her into his care. Said they had a deep, loving relationship and that he would take responsibility for her rehabilitation."

"But Stephanie wasn't taken in by him?"

"As I said, Stephanie may be many things, but she's not a fool. George, my brother-in-law, called the police to see Strasser off the premises, and then Stephanie rang me to see what I could find out about him."

Jason pointed to the file in front of her. "And that's what you found out?"

"So far," Violet said. "But I have a feeling I've only just scratched the surface."

"What are we going to do about it?"

"Well, we're not going to go up against him alone. We played that game last time, and we didn't do very well, did we?"

"So what do you suggest?"

"We ask the professionals to get involved."

"The police?"

She made a sound of contempt in the back of her throat. "They wouldn't know where to start."

"Then who?"

"I want you to go and see a man I know, Harry Bailey. I helped him with something he was investigating a few years ago."

"Who's this Harry Bailey?"

"He works for Department 18. A government agency set up to investigate psychic phenomena, the paranormal."

"'The government uses taxpayers' money to investigate ghoulies and ghosties?" Jason said incredulously. "I'm surprised the *Daily Mail* hasn't tried to expose them and bring them down."

"They operate below the radar of the popular press, and believe me, they've saved the country's bacon on more than one occasion."

"Seriously?"

"Jason, I'm deadly serious. I never joke about such things."

Jason saw the steely look in her eyes and backed off

"We're not the only ones who see the evil in the souls of men and others."

"Okay, Vi, where do I find this Harry Bailey?"

"You're meeting with him in the morning in a café on the Euston Road. I called him earlier. He'll meet with you at nine. Miguel's. It's almost opposite King's Cross Station."

"How will I know him?"

"He'll know you. He's heard of you and knows what you look like."

"How?"

She looked at him and a slight smile played on her lips. "You're quite famous, Jason. Your beating made the front page of the *Evening Standard*, although they fudged the details somewhat. Put it down as a mugging. If they only knew."

"Best they don't. But I had no idea I'd made the press." He looked unhappy. "Why don't you meet with him yourself?"

"I will, eventually, but at the moment he thinks I'm more use here, digging up as much information on Strasser as I can find. He'll do the same at his end. He has access to some top-class researchers. I'll meet up with him soon, but for now you take this file, read it, digest it, meet with Harry, give it to him and see if he plans to do anything about it."

"You think he might not?"

She closed the file and handed it across the desk to him. "He'll take it on. He wouldn't be Harry Bailey if he didn't. Report back to me once you've met with him."

With the file tucked under his arm, Jason left the library, walked the length of Violet's vast Chelsea home and stepped out into the evening air.

Chapter Three

Miguel's was a place out of time and soon to be swallowed up and consigned to oblivion by the King's Cross redevelopment program. The current owner, a Cypriot called Theo, had enjoyed twenty years in the area, but was resigned to the reality of his situation. His café was an anachronism now, as much as Eddie the barber's three doors down. Soon they would be no more. In the months to come, Miguel's would be replaced by a Starbucks or a Costa, and another facet of London's rich heritage would cease to shine.

Jason West stepped in out of the drizzling rain and wiped the moisture droplets from his raincoat.

"What can I get you?" Theo asked him in heavily accented English.

"Just tea, please," Jason said.

"I'll bring it over. Take a seat…if you can find one."

Jason looked around the deserted café and admired the man's stoic irony. "You're very quiet," he said.

"You missed the breakfast rush. It will be dead in here until twelve. Then all hell breaks loose as the secretaries start to come in for their lunch. I can cope. My staff will arrive soon."

Jason wandered over to a table in the window, sat and opened the newspaper he was carrying. Theo brought his tea in a cup that resembled a soup bowl with a handle and set it down it on the table in front of him. A few moments later the door swung inward and a large man with graying hair and a beaten-up-looking face stepped into the café and went through the ritual of wiping raindrops from his raincoat.

"Harry!" Theo called from behind the counter. "Your usual?"

The big man finished wiping himself down. "Just tea and toast, Theo. I'm in a bit of a rush this morning." He looked across to Jason, who was folding his newspaper and laying it on the seat beside him. "May I join you?" he said.

Jason looked up at him. "Feel free."

The man pulled a chair from under the table and sat down opposite him. "Harry Bailey," he said.

Jason stuck out a hand. "West. Jason West."

"Yeah, I know," Harry said, taking his hand and shaking it. "How's Vi?"

"Fine. Fully recovered now."

"You were lucky—you both were."

"Yes, I realize that."

Theo brought across another bowl of tea and a plate holding two slices of thickly buttered toast. Harry nodded his thanks, picked up a slice of toast and bit into it, wiping his chin with the back of his hand as melted butter ran down from the corners of his mouth. He spoke as he chewed. "Vi told me what you're here for, and, I'm afraid to say, I don't think the department can help you."

Jason sipped his tea. "Then it was a bit of a waste of time meeting up with you. Vi was convinced you'd help her," he said, an edge of irritation in his voice.

Harry took another bite of toast, wiped his chin again. "Don't get chippy. I said I don't think Department 18 can help you. I didn't say *I* wouldn't. I've known Violet Bulmer for a long time. She's a friend. I've always got time to help out my friends."

"So why won't the department get involved?"

Harry washed down the toast with a mouthful of tea. "My boss won't sanction it."

Jason pulled a manila folder from the inside pocket of his coat. "Erik Strasser is a dangerous man." He offered the file to Harry.

Harry took it, laid it down on the table next to his plate but didn't open it. "I'm sure he is. But my boss would say that this—" he tapped the file, "—falls into the category of cranks and weirdos, not a paranormal threat as such."

"But he runs a coven, here in London."

"And what's a coven but a collection of cranks and weirdos? There's nothing the department can do unless it's shown that Strasser and his followers present some kind of danger to the public."

"Vi told you about her niece?"

"Yes, she told me. Very sad, and I can imagine Vi's anger, but again, there's no overt supernatural threat there, just a misguided girl falling in with the wrong crowd. She might have joined the Moonies or even the Scientologists, makes no difference. It's still outside the department's remit."

"So what *can* you do?"

Harry picked up the file, folded it in half and slipped it into his pocket. "Leave this with me. I'll read it and get my people to look at it and see what we can come up with." He took a last mouthful of toast and another swig of tea and got to his feet.

"And that's the best you can do?" Jason said.

"It's more than most people would get, but it's Vi, and she's a good woman, working on the side of the angels. I'll help her. Where can I reach you?"

Jason took a pen from his pocket, picked up his newspaper and scribbled a number in the margin. "It's my cell. You can get me anytime."

Harry took the paper and slipped it under his arm. "I'll be in touch," he said, went to the counter to pay for his breakfast and slipped back out into the drizzle.

Jason drained the last of his tea from his cup and set it back on its saucer. Theo glanced across at him. "Can I get you another?"

"No thanks. I'll just pay for the one I had."

"No need. Mr. Bailey paid for you both."

"Well, at least I got something to compensate for the early start."

"Eh?"

Jason shook his head. "It doesn't matter," he said.

As he was leaving the café, an elderly woman with tightly permed hair, and wearing a plastic mac, pushed through the door and took a position behind the counter. The staff, Jason surmised with a wry smile.

"Erik Strasser," Martin Impey said. "Doesn't ring any bells."

Harry Bailey dropped the file Jason West had given him onto Martin's desk. "Do some digging," he said. "See if you can add any more to that."

"What are you looking for?

"Something, anything I can use to justify a full department investigation."

"Going out on a limb again, Harry?"

"A favor for a friend. So keep it quiet…for now."

Martin picked up the file and started leafing through it. "As you wish. I'll call you if I find anything."

"Top man," Harry said and went back to his own office.

Chapter Four

"What are you up to, Harry?" Jane Talbot said as she passed him in the corridor leading to the offices.

"What makes you think I'm up to anything?"

"You look furtive."

"Ha!" Harry laughed. "That's the first time I've ever been called *furtive*."

"Well, you do."

Harry took her arm and guided her into an empty office. "Do you have a moment?"

"You see? Furtive."

"You know this place, Jane. Worse than the Whispering Gallery in St Paul's."

"Be quick, Harry," she said. "Rob's waiting for me in the car park. We have an assignment over the bridge in Croydon." Robert Carter was Jane Talbot's partner, both at work and in life. Their on-again, off-again relationship had been an ongoing department saga for some years now. It was frowned upon by Simon Crozier, Department 18's director in chief, but they ignored his nonfraternization of staff edict, carried on regardless, and there wasn't a damned thing he could do about it—not if he wanted them to remain on the department's payroll. And they were too good at their jobs for him to lose them. So Crozier grumbled and frowned and made their lives as difficult as possible. It made for a colorful working environment.

"Erik Strasser," Harry said. "Heard of him?"

Jane shrugged. "The name means nothing to me."

"No. It meant nothing to me until last night, but he sounds like a real piece of work. Heads a coven based in Docklands. Targets young people as his followers, and sets about destroying them, getting them hooked on drugs, that kind of stuff."

"So how does that interest us? Covens and cults are ten a penny. We don't get involved."

"That's what I told her, and her partner."

"Told who?"

"Violet Bulmer."

"Vi? When did she resurface? I thought that incident with the Suffolk Residual finished her off."

"And it nearly did. Why she and her partner decided to tackle it alone, I'll never know. Damned near killed the both of them. She was in hospital for three weeks."

"And her partner?"

"Nearer six. He's very young. Completely out of his depth. Jason West. Bit of a gunslinger."

"Oh dear," Jane said. "I remember Rob being like that once."

"And me, years ago, but we learned to keep our powder dry. Maybe West will…one day."

"And Vi's got you involved in this Erik Strasser thing. What's she running, her own private investigation?"

"Strasser got his hands on Vi's niece. A pure corruption attempt by all accounts. Got her hooked on crystal meth, probably used her body as well—although Vi was a bit reticent on that aspect, but I know Strasser's kind. They're usually narcissists with a God complex. Probably impotent and compensating for it."

"And the girl? Vi's niece."

"In a Hampshire clinic. Safe for now."

"So what does Vi want from you?"

"She's going to bring Strasser down, so what happened to her niece can't happen to anyone else."

"As I said, Harry, it's not what we do. Simon would have a pink fit if he knew you were even contemplating getting involved."

"So we don't tell him. It wouldn't be the first time. Have a word with Rob, when you see him. See if he's heard of Erik Strasser, and sound him out about lending a hand."

"Oh, he'll be up for it. Anything to piss off Simon. You know Rob."

Harry grinned. "I thought you might say that. And you?"

"Where my beloved goes, I follow, I guess."

Harry threw a playful punch at her arm. "Knew I could rely on you," he said.

The Mayberry Clinic stood in its own grounds in an area free of trees in the middle of the New Forest, a sprawling redbrick mansion with a gray slate roof. The house had adopted many identities since it was built in the mid-nineteenth century—a grand family home, a girls' preparatory school, an hotel and, for five years back in the 1970s, a remand home for wayward teens. That was when they installed the metal grilles at the ornate mullioned windows. When the Mayberry Clinic took over the lease in the early 2000s, they saw no reason to remove the metalwork at the windows. So Alice Logan's view of the rolling grounds and the forest beyond was marred by perpendicular, closely spaced bars, and by the steady spatter of rain bouncing from the glass.

"I was talking to you, Alice." It was a woman's voice, Dr. Tayeb, the clinic's senior behavioral psychologist.

"I'm watching the rain," Alice said, but she'd been sedated and her words were slurring, making it come out as "Swashingrain."

"Do you like watching the rain, Alice?" Shahneelah Tayeb asked her.

"Sbritty."

"Yes, Alice. It *is* pretty. Perhaps you can go outside and take a walk in the pretty rain…later."

"He's coming for me," Alice said in little more than a whisper, the words clear, no slurring.

"Sorry, Alice. Who's coming for you?"

Alice put a finger to her lips, flattening the smile that had just settled there. "Ssshhh. Secret."

"No secrets, Alice. We agreed."

"Yes, I can hear you. I'll be ready.'

"Alice?" And then Shahneelah Tayeb realized Alice wasn't addressing her. The girl's head was cocked to one side, and her attention was again being drawn to the window.

The door to the room opened and a nurse entered, carrying a small tray. On the tray were a glass of water and a small plastic beaker containing two white pills.

Dr. Tayeb looked round furiously at the rather plain young woman with the shock of orange hair pinned precariously under the starched white cap. "Not now, nurse. I'm in the middle of an interview."

The nurse carried on into the room. "Time for Miss Logan's medication," she said, and regarded the psychologist with sullen eyes.

"I said, not now."

Alice watched the exchange incuriously, and then she said, "He's here."

Before Dr. Tayeb could respond, the nurse dropped the tray. It landed with a crash, the glass shattering on the parquet floor, the pills spilling from the beaker and rolling under the bed. "Nurse?" she said. But the young woman didn't hear her. She stared at the window as the blood drained from her sallow, plain face, and then she fell to the floor, her body twitching.

"Nurse?" Dr. Tayeb said again, and moved forward to assist the fallen woman, but froze as her air supply was suddenly cut off.

Her eyes widened and her hands went to her throat, but it was no use. She couldn't draw in a breath. Equally she couldn't expel any air from her lungs, and her body reacted, going into spasm as her chest heaved, trying desperately to suck in some air. Blood was popping in her ears and her head began to pound.

She threw out her arms, windmilling them as she tried to regain control of her breathing, but her throat was blocked. The room was swimming, bed and furniture blurring before her eyes. The last thing she saw before pitching forward, face-first onto the hard, unyielding floor, was Alice's almost serene smile.

As Tayeb's mouth crashed down on the parquet, shattering her front teeth and splitting her lips, pain exploded in her head. Had she been able to draw in her breath, she would have screamed, but all she could manage was a thin squeak of sound as a black cloak fluttered down over her eyes and her heart stopped.

At 10.37 a.m., Shahneelah Tayeb died. The nurse stopped twitching a few seconds later, and died as her brain dissolved inside her skull.

Alice Logan looked down at the two women lying on the floor. "Well, that's that," she said quietly to herself before walking calmly to the door and letting herself out of the room.

She walked through the house unchallenged, no one giving her more than a casual glance. At the front door she paused and looked back, but again nobody said anything to her—the middle-aged woman at the reception desk was more concerned with the argument she was having on the phone with her husband, who'd gone shopping to the local supermarket and forgotten to buy cat food.

Alice opened one of the doors and slipped outside, pulling it shut behind her. There was a gunmetal-gray Lexus parked on the gravel drive. She went across to it and pulled open the passenger door.

Erik Strasser sat behind the wheel. As she slid in next to him, he took her hand and squeezed it reassuringly. "Well, my darling Hecate. I think we should leave."

Alice smiled at him. "Yes, I think I'd like that."

He started the car, put it into drive and eased the car slowly over the gravel and forward towards the main gates. Seconds later they were heading out on the only road through the trees of the New Forest, towards the main road to London.

"Vi, what do you mean gone?" Harry Bailey barked into the phone.

"The clinic just telephoned me. Alice has disappeared. The doctor who was treating her and a nurse are both dead."

"Did she kill them?"

"I don't know. I'm driving down there now. I want some answers."

Harry checked his watch. "Give me the address. I'll meet you there."

Violet Bulmer read out the address of the clinic, her voice a flat monotone. The news had obviously knocked her for six.

"It's a three-hour drive," Harry said. "Can you handle that?"

"I'll get Jason to drive me," she said. "I'll see you there. And, Harry."

"Yes?"

"Thanks."

Chapter Five

Dr. Richard Frost met them at the doors to the clinic when they arrived. "Perhaps you'd like to come through to my office," he said, and led them through the foyer to a brightly lit corridor. The door at the end bore his name, embossed on a brass plaque.

Harry and Violet followed him into the room. Jason West had elected to find a gas station and fill up the car in preparation for the journey home.

Frost arranged two chairs at the large oak desk, opposite his own, and gestured for them to sit. He was a tall, elegant man who wore his Paul Smith suit as a symbol of his prosperity and authority. It hugged his slim frame like a second skin, and he adjusted his trousers as he sat and crossed his legs. "I spoke to Mrs. Logan this morning to apprise her of the situation," he said. "She advised me you'd be down to see me. I assume you're her sister."

"Indeed," Violet said. "Stephanie is my sister. Alice, my niece."

Frost looked from her to Harry, the unasked question evident in his eyes.

"Harry Bailey." He stretched out a hand across the desk. "A family friend," he added. He had his Department 18 identity card in his pocket, but would only produce it if absolutely necessary. This was still not official department business. Just a friendly gesture, so far.

Frost seemed to take the explanation of his identity at face value, shook Harry's hand and relaxed back into his chair. "This is all very unfortunate," he said. "It's never happened before."

"Patients don't usually walk out then?" Harry said.

Frost shook his head. "Most of our guests are here of their own volition.

They have no reason to leave. They're here to seek our help. Walking out rather defeats that objective." He smiled. Frost was an immensely likable man with an open, kind face with reassuring gray eyes, and Harry found himself warming to him. The first impression of a pedant was dismissed.

"You say guests, not patients," Violet said. "Yet you call yourself a clinic. How does that work?"

"As I say, people usually come here voluntarily. They have a problem, and they come to us to help them deal with it. So I, and my staff, refer to them and treat them like guests. We find it's more conducive to helping them in their attempts to cope with their difficulties."

"And yet you have bars on your windows," Harry said.

"A hangover from one of the building's earlier incarnations. There was a plan to remove them, but we found they actually reassure our guests; the bars give them an added sense of security."

"But to someone not here voluntarily, they would represent a prison," Violet said.

Frost slowly nodded his head. "As in the case of your niece. Yes, I *do* see that, and I was reluctant to have her here. But I've known Lawrence O'Connell, Alice's doctor, since university. I agreed to take her in because the situation seemed so desperate, and I have had experience dealing with people who have a dependency on methamphetamine. With the benefit of hindsight, I realize it was the wrong decision." Frost's eyes dimmed and it was obvious what had happened was troubling him greatly.

"The two members of your staff who were the last to see Alice before she walked out of here, how did they die?" Harry said.

"Was Alice responsible for their deaths?" Violet added.

Frost shook his head. "I can't say. I'm awaiting the results of the postmortems. They were both taken to Bournemouth General. There's a Home Office pathologist on his way down from London to perform them."

"The Home Office is involved?" Harry said. His surprise was evident.

"I'm afraid we had to involve the police when Alice walked out. They are treating the deaths of Dr. Tayeb and Nurse Williams as suspicious. A Home Office pathologist is always called in such circumstances," Frost said and looked to Violet, who had shifted uncomfortably in her seat. "I'm sorry, but I'm afraid your niece was a methamphetamine addict, and those hooked on crystal meth do have a tendency towards aggressive behavior."

"Did Alice attack the nurse and the doctor?" Violet asked.

"I did the preliminary examinations and there wasn't a mark on either of them," Frost said.

"So how do you think they died?" Harry said.

"As I said, we won't know anything—"

"Until you get the results of the postmortem. Yes, I get that, but you're a doctor. You must have some idea, if it's only a gut feeling."

It was Frost's turn to shift in his seat. "It looked to me like Shahneelah, Dr. Tayeb, choked on her own tongue. It rarely happens, but it can in extreme circumstances, convulsions and suchlike. In the doctor's case it looked as though her tongue had been forced back down her throat, blocking her windpipe completely and cutting off her air supply."

Violet shuddered. "And the nurse?"

"She simply stopped. At first I suspected a heart attack, but there was bleeding from her ears and nose, which leads me to think now that it might have been a cerebral hemorrhage or something similar. I don't know. I'm afraid that's out of my area of expertise."

As the conversation went on, Frost was looking less and less comfortable. Harry was surprised that the doctor had already been so candid with them. Most people in his situation would have clammed up completely for fear of lawsuits. It seemed Richard Frost was grateful to have someone to share the burden with.

"What are the police doing about Alice?" Violet asked.

"They're looking for her. Not as someone who has walked out of here, you understand—our guests are free to come and go as they please; they're not legally obliged to stay here—but they want to interview Alice in connection with Dr. Tayeb's and Nurse Williams's deaths."

"What a bloody mess," Violet said under her breath, but Frost heard her.

"Yes," he said. "An absolute bloody mess. I'm sorry."

"How did she seem, Alice, while she was here?" Harry said.

"I interviewed her when she first arrived. She seemed like a sweet girl, placid, docile. I certainly didn't see that she could be a threat to my staff. It's why this business has me shocked and baffled. Believe it or not, I'm pretty good at reading people."

"I believe you," Harry said. "Was there anything about her behavior, anything she said or did that struck you as unusual?"

Frost leaned back in his chair, steepled his fingers and blew across the tops of them as he considered Harry's question. After a moment he said, "One thing she said, and she said it more than once, 'He won't let me stay here. He'll come for me'."

"Any idea who she was talking about?"

"Lawrence told me that Alice had been involved with someone, a man, a bad influence, who might have instigated her meth addiction. Alice could have been talking about him."

"Did she give you a name?" Violet said.

Frost shook his head. "Lawrence didn't know his name. But it seems Alice had formed quite a close bond with him…whoever he was."

Harry got to his feet. "I think we're done here, Vi," he said.

"I hope I've been of some help," Frost said.

Violet stood. "Yes, Dr. Frost. A great help. Perhaps you'll let us know as soon as you hear anything from the police."

"Of course."

"And the pathologist," Harry said.

Frost looked doubtful. "I'm not sure I can do that. There will be an inquest. I'm sure everything will come to light then."

Harry nodded. He wasn't going to pressure him—couldn't without the backing of the department, and to get that he'd have to make Alice's case official, and he wasn't ready to do that.

"Fair enough. Thank you for your time, Dr. Frost. If you remember anything else or can tell us anything that might help us find Alice, perhaps you would give me a call." Harry handed the doctor his personal card and watched with satisfaction as the man read it and slipped it into the top pocket of his jacket.

Jason West was leaning against the hood of the car, smoking a cigarette. As Harry and Violet emerged from the clinic, he dropped the butt, and ground it under the heel of his shoe.

Violet turned to Harry and hugged him. "See you back at mine?"

"Yes." Harry kissed her cheek and walked to his own car parked alongside hers. "We'll talk when we get back."

"You'll stay for lunch?"

Harry nodded, climbed in behind the wheel and started the engine.

"Well?" Jason said as Violet slipped into the car beside him.

"I'll tell you about it as we drive." She looked back at the clinic and gave an involuntary shudder.

"Are you okay?" Jason said.

"A gray goose just walked over my grave," she said.

Jason looked at her askance, but said nothing as he drove out through the gates of the clinic, back down to the main road.

Chapter Six

Strasser carried a mug of coffee into the bedroom and set it down on the nightstand, and then he leaned over the bed and kissed Alice on the cheek. "Wake up," he said softly. "It's late."

Alice Logan's eyes fluttered open, and she ran a hand across her scalp, twining her hair between her fingers as she looked across at the digital clock on the bedside cabinet. It read 17.30. "You shouldn't have let me sleep so long."

Strasser shrugged. "You needed it. Drink your coffee.'

"Sleep isn't what I need, nor is coffee. You know what I need."

"Later," he said gently.

"Now." She propped herself up onto one elbow. "Now, Erik," she insisted.

He regarded her for a moment, and then pulled something from his pocket. "You really shouldn't be taking this anymore."

She said nothing but stuck out her hand.

He shrugged again and dropped the suppository into her outstretched palm. She threw back the covers, swung her feet to the floor and padded naked across to the bathroom. When she returned she looked more awake, but her eyes were glittery, slightly manic.

Strasser was sitting on the bed. He would have to stop dosing her soon. The meth was starting to affect her looks. She had aged five years in the last three months. He should never have got her hooked, but it was the only way. "Shower and get dressed," he said. "We have to go out."

She flopped back down on the bed and spread her legs. "Fuck me first."

Strasser smiled. "That's an invitation I wouldn't usually refuse, but we have to be somewhere soon. Take a shower…and drink your coffee. And get dressed."

The corners of her mouth turned downwards in a pout and she thrust her hand between her legs. "But I need you, Erik."

"You need coffee." He stood up from the bed and walked from the bedroom, letting the door swing shut behind him.

"Bastard!" she called after him, took the coffee mug from the cabinet and hurled it against the closing door. And then she began to cry.

Thirty minutes later she was showered and dressed. She walked into the lounge and stood in the doorway, wanting him to show his approval, but her thoughts were beginning to blur and jumble as the crystal meth worked its insidious way to her brain, and she started to sway.

He sat on the larger of the two couches in the sparsely furnished room, flicking through a magazine. He looked up at her, taking in her silky blonde hair and small breasts pushing against the lemon silk of her blouse. He stood up and went across to her, holding her by the shoulders to stop her swaying. "Beautiful," he said. "Shall we go?"

Harry hated driving through London, hated Chelsea even more. He reached Violet's house and pulled in behind her dark green Honda. They had beaten him back from Bournemouth.

Jason answered the door at the first ring and ushered him inside. Violet was in her usual position, seated behind the desk in the library. She was always in the library when he met her. He couldn't recall ever being in any other room of the house.

"Well," she said, as he entered the library. "What did you make of Dr. Frost?"

Harry sat down at the desk. "Unusually open. I liked him."

"Yes. He certainly didn't try to hide anything, at least not that I could read from his aura."

"Do you think Alice could be responsible for the doctor and nurse?"

Violet shook her head. "Not Alice. Strasser maybe."

Jason joined them at the desk. "Most likely," he said. "Strasser heads a coven. He probably used witchcraft to get them out of the way while Alice escaped."

"We need to find out more about him if we ever want to get Alice back," Violet said.

"Do you think he has her?" Harry said.

Violet snorted. "What do you think? 'He's coming for me…he won't let me stay here.'" she quoted. "She must have been talking about Strasser."

"I think that's the most likely scenario," Jason said. "From what I read in his file, Strasser seems utterly ruthless and determined to get what he wants."

"I phoned Martin Impey, my researcher at the department," Harry said. "He's starting to compile his own file on our Mr. Strasser. He told me a few of the things he's found out about him. I think you're right, Jason. He's setting something up, and whatever it is, Alice has a role to play. I don't think your sister's plan to spirit her away and hide her at the clinic will have fazed him at all, Vi. He tends to get what he wants, whatever the cost."

Dark clouds scudded across Violet's eyes and she slammed her hand down on the desk. The two men looked at her, startled. It was unusual for her to show any outward sign of emotion, but Alice's abduction had her rattled. "We've got to get her back, away from this monster." Tears were welling in her eyes. "I used to change her nappy, for Christ's sake, push her on the swing that hung from the oak tree in the garden. She's like my own daughter."

Harry reached across the desk and laid his hand over hers. "We'll get her back, Vi, I promise."

She looked at him bleakly. "You shouldn't make promises you can't keep, Harry."

"What if I promise as well?" Jason said.

Violet shot him a disparaging look, and then she shook herself as she tried to get her emotions under control. "I'm sorry. I know you both mean well, but what can we do?"

"I think it's time we made this an official Department 18 investigation. Use all their resources," Harry said.

"But I thought you said your boss would never go for it," Violet said.

"That was when you first told me about it. Circumstances have changed now. Dr. Tayeb and Nurse Williams have been killed and Alice is still missing. I don't think even Simon Crozier would deny us the right to look into it. He's sanctioned assignments for less. Let me speak with him." He got to his feet. "I'll call you as soon as I have. Later today, okay?"

Violet reached out her hand and grabbed his, squeezing it tightly. "Thanks, Harry."

"Do you think a full Department 18 investigation is appropriate at this time, Harry?" Simon Crozier said, and wiped a stray fingerprint from the surface of his smoked glass desk with the sleeve of his jacket.

Harry regarded him for a moment. "Totally appropriate. Two people have been killed and the girl is still missing. More importantly it's Vi Bulmer's niece, and as you well know, Vi's a friend of the department. She's helped us immeasurably in the past. We owe her."

Crozier slowly nodded his head. "I agree that Violet Bulmer has been a great asset over the years, but I'm just concerned that your objectivity might be compromised by your personal feelings for her."

"Bollocks!" Harry exploded. "You know me better than that. Why do you have to turn everything into a battle, Simon? I should have come to you when Vi first called me, but I didn't because I knew what your reaction would be."

"Which is?"

"*This.* Weighing up the severity of a case with one eye on the purse strings."

"Careful, Harry. I don't have to take that, not even from one of my oldest friends. Of course I'm concerned about Violet's niece, but this Strasser person, what evidence do you have that he's not just a crank?"

"The doctor and nurse at the clinic for a start."

"But you're still waiting for the results of the postmortem. You have no evidence that Strasser was in any way involved. The nurse could have died from a brain hemorrhage and the doctor choked on her own tongue. Both could be classified as natural causes. There's no evidence of a paranormal attack."

"Apart from the fact that they were both healthy young women who seemed to have dropped dead within minutes of each other. Circumstances that could only benefit Strasser."

Crozier seemed to flinch. "Well, put like that…"

"Let me pull a team together to go after Strasser and return Alice Logan to her family."

Crozier took a deep breath, held it for a moment, and then blew it out through his lips. "Very well, Harry. Do that, but bear in mind, although you might not like it, books have to be balanced and funding for the department comes under scrutiny by the Select Committee next month. I'm expected to justify our budget and account for every penny. Don't let this investigation turn into a three-ring circus."

"I'll be circumspect," Harry said.

"Well, I suppose there's a first time for everything. Go on, get out of here and assemble your team. Keep me in the loop."

Harry grinned and made for the door.

"And, Harry, give Violet Bulmer my best wishes."

"Vi? Simon Crozier's agreed to full Department 18 involvement." Harry leaned against the wall in the corridor and spoke into his cell phone.

"That's marvelous, Harry. Thank you so much. So what happens next?"

"I'm going to put together a team to go after Strasser. I want to take his life apart and see what makes him tick. See why he needs Alice. As I said, this kind of crank usually has a plan."

"What do you mean?"

"There's usually something behind what they do. World domination, raising Satan, bringing the Antichrist back to earth… There's usually some kind of grandiose plan. These people tend to think in clichés. We need to find out what's behind Strasser's personal cliché."

"You *are* taking him seriously?" Violet sounded concerned.

"Even people without an ounce of original thought can be dangerous and need to be taken seriously," Harry said. "You never know, Strasser might surprise us and come up with something new."

"Is there anything I can do in the meantime?"

"Keep digging," Harry said. "Impey and his team are good—the best—but I know what you are capable of. You might uncover something. And I want your boy Jason on the team. I've kept an eye on him over the years. He may be a bit of a cowboy, but he's dedicated and very capable."

"Shall I ask him to meet with you in Whitehall?"

"Yes, send him along. One other thing, I want to go and see your sister."

"Stephanie? Why?"

"I need to find out more about Alice. Your sister's best placed to tell me all about her."

"I'll arrange for you to meet with her."

"As soon as possible."

"I'll call her now and fix it up. I'll call you back."

"Oh, and Simon Crozier sends his best wishes."

"I don't know Simon Crozier. Only what you've told me about him."

"But he knows of you, and he's aware of the help you've given us in the past. He may be a pompous prick sometimes, but I believe his heart's in the right place."

"Thank him for me, Harry. I really appreciate this."

"He knows, but I'll send your thanks anyway."

Jason West knocked on the door to Harry's office and stood, tapping his foot, waiting to be called in. Instead the door was pulled open and Harry stood there, tie askew, sweat staining a shirt that was a stranger to an iron. Crumbs from the sandwich he was holding peppered his mouth. "Jason," he said. "Good of you to come over so quickly." He lifted the hand holding the sandwich. "Sorry about this. I picked it up from the service station at Membury and haven't had a chance to eat it until now. I finally had to give in to my ulcer. It gives me hell if I don't feed it."

Jason stepped into the cluttered office. With curly brown hair creeping over the collar of his denim jacket and gold studs through the lobes of each ear, he looked more like a fairground roustabout than a serious psychic investigator. That was why Harry Bailey liked him and wanted him on his team. It was good to have people around him who didn't conform. They were more likely to think *out of the box*.

"And are you?" Harry said.

"Am I what?"

"Romany. You look Romany. Didn't I say?"

"No."

"Well, I was thinking it. Are you?"

Jason smiled. "On my mother's side, yes."

"Thought so." Harry beamed. "Good instincts, the gypsies. You don't mind that term?"

Jason shook his head. "I've been called worse," he said. "Vi said we're fighting the clock, so I thought I'd better get over here straight away."

"Quite right. No time to lose. She's just phoned me and arranged for us to meet her sister this evening. Are you up for it? It means a drive over to Hertfordshire. I shouldn't think we'll get back until after the pubs shut."

"That's not a problem. I don't drink."

"Nor me," Harry said.

"Do you have a problem with it?"

"I like it too much. That's the problem I have with it. Anyway, let's not drag our feet. Stephanie Logan is expecting us."

"I thought I was here to meet the people in your team."

"And so you shall. Tomorrow maybe. When I've chosen them."

Chapter Seven

Stephanie Logan's house was nothing out of the ordinary: a neat three-story townhouse, set in the leafy Hertfordshire town of Hitchin. They pulled up in the street outside, under a sodium street lamp that cast an orange glow over the front gardens. They got out of the car and stood looking at the house.

"Not what I was expecting," Jason said.

"Really?"

"Well, Vi's place is probably worth six times more than this. I suppose I was expecting something similar."

"Vi married well. Francis Bulmer was a big noise in the city," Harry said.

"I didn't know Vi was married—she never mentioned a husband."

"No, she's a widow," Harry said. "Frank Bulmer died the year after they married, and Vi copped the entire estate. It's why she doesn't work. She doesn't need to."

"I wondered. How long have you known her?"

"Long enough. Anyway, let's crack on. I'll tell you about Vi and me another time." Harry strode up the path and pressed the doorbell.

The woman who answered the door and introduced herself as Stephanie Logan surprised Jason as much as where she lived. Fine boned and smartly dressed in a gray business suit, an expensive haircut and a string of pearls at her throat, Stephanie Logan seemed to be the opposite of Violet Bulmer in every way.

"Won't you come in?" she said with clipped enunciation, although Jason could detect a fragility in her voice that seemed at odds with her appearance.

She led them inside and along a luxuriously carpeted hall, bringing them to a halt in a room that looked as if it had been lifted from the pages of *Good Housekeeping* magazine.

"Please take a seat. George will join us shortly. He's just taking a shower."

George was evidently her husband, judging from the framed photograph that hung on the wall above the fireplace. A group shot, printed onto canvas, of Stephanie, a serious-looking but mildly handsome man in his forties and, lounging at their feet, a very pretty teenager with blonde hair cloaking her shoulders, vibrant blue eyes and a smile to melt the hardest of hearts. Flanking them was a young man, about the same age as Alice. As good-looking as the rest of the family, but his looks marred by a slightly sneering expression that he wore on his face like a badge of honor.

"Alice?" Harry said, indicating the family portrait.

"Yes." Stephanie nodded. "My husband, George, and Tim, our son. Alice's brother. Taken in happier times," she added wistfully. "Please take a seat. Coffee?"

"Tea for me, if it's no trouble," Jason said. "Three sugars."

Stephanie's eyebrows rose a few millimeters but she said, "Yes, of course. No trouble at all."

"Coffee for me," Harry said. "Black. No sugar."

As she came back a little while later, George Logan followed her into the room and introduced himself. Stephanie laid the tray of tea and coffee down onto a low glass-topped table and began to pour coffee from a glass-and-chrome cafetière.

Harry found his eyes drifting to the photograph once more. How a family's life could be turned on its head. He felt a growing anger towards Erik Strasser.

"Happier times," George said. He too was staring at the photo.

"Yes, your wife said. It's a lovely portrait. Alice is a very pretty girl."

"And so happy…" Stephanie said. "At least she was. When she came back to us recently, she was a mere shadow of the girl there. We really do appreciate you helping us with this. The police are bloody useless; no help at all. As far as they're concerned, she's above the age of consent, and if she chooses to go off and live with someone, that's up to her. They say there's not a lot they can do about it.

Bastards!" she added, her voice rising.

"Stephanie." George reached across and squeezed her knee. "Don't upset yourself."

"Don't patronize me," she snapped at her husband. "If you'd been more a father to her instead of wanting to be her best friend, shown her a little more discipline, none of this might have happened."

George's mouth opened to protest, but nothing came out. He seemed to sink into himself and buried his face in his hands. His shoulders heaved once and he took his hands away from his face. "Growing up, she was a good girl. Never gave us any trouble. She got good grades at school. Even made it through to Oxford on sheer hard work. We were so proud of her."

He was cut off by the sound of the front door opening and crashing shut.

Stephanie glanced round. "Tim? Is that you?"

A young man lurched into the lounge, dressed in biker's leathers and carrying a crash helmet. He flopped down into an armchair and put his feet up on the coffee table, which earned him a stern look from his father.

"As I was saying," George continued. "Alice never gave us any trouble. Quiet and studious, but bright and vivacious when she wanted to be, she was doing well at university. Glowing testimonials from her tutors. She was heavily tipped to get an honors degree. From then it would be forward onto her doctorate."

"What was she reading?" Jason asked, his eyes fixed on Alice's brother, who was wearing the same slightly sneering expression he'd perfected for the family portrait. He was staring down at his knees as if he'd heard all this before and wasn't interested in the slightest.

"Classical studies, specializing in both ancient Greece and Greek mythology. It was her passion. I suppose that's why she was so good at it."

Tim Logan reached into the pocket of his leather jacket and pulled out a packet of cigarettes. He took one out and placed it between his lips.

"Not in the house!" Stephanie snapped before he could reach for a lighter. Tim swore under his breath, took the cigarette from his mouth and got to his feet. "I'll smoke it in the garden. Any objection to me polluting the air outside?" he said and walked out of the room.

Stephanie shook her head sadly but said nothing as she watched him walk away.

Jason got to his feet and took his own cigarettes from his pocket. "I'll keep him company," he said. "If you don't mind."

George shook his head; Stephanie sniffed disdainfully. Harry avoided Jason's eyes.

When he'd left the room, Harry said, "When did you notice a change in Alice's behavior?"

"When she came back for the Easter break," Stephanie said. "I knew immediately something was wrong."

Tim Logan glanced around when Jason stepped out into the garden. His cigarette was already lit and he was puffing at it furiously. "You're not a worshipper then?"

"Sorry?" Jason said. He lit his own cigarette and blew smoke up at the night sky.

"Kneeling at the altar of Saint Alice of Hitchin. It's the new religion around here."

Jason smiled. "Is that how you see her? Saint Alice?"

"It's how *they* see her. If they only knew."

Jason walked across to an ornamental fishpond with a low, rough-stone wall. A rather ugly statue of Dionysus stood in the center of the pond, water dribbling over the bunch of grapes he held aloft in his right hand.

"He had the right idea," Tim said, coming up behind him. "Get pissed and stay pissed. The only way to live."

"Did you get on well with Alice?"

"Well enough, considering the age gap."

"Age gap? How big?"

"She's three minutes older than me. I'm the younger brother, and I've been treated as such for as long as I can remember. We're twins, but not identical. She got the brains, you see."

"What did you get?"

"I got the leftovers. In their eyes I've always been the *also ran*."

Jason gave him a sympathetic look. "It happens in families. Glad I was an only child." He dipped the glowing end of his half-smoked cigarette in the pond and lit another, offering the pack to the boy. Tim Logan dropped his own stub to the ground and took a cigarette from Jason with a nod of thanks.

"But apart from that, you got on with her okay," Jason said as he lit the boy's cigarette with his Zippo.

Tim inhaled deeply and let the smoke dribble out through his nose. "Yeah," he said. "Ally was fun. Mad as a box of frogs, but fun. We had some good times before she went to uni."

"Did she change when she went up to Oxford?"

"Not at first. I remember the first summer she came home. We caught a train to Cambridge together and went punting on the Cam. It was a blast. We stopped for lunch at a pub. Mum and Dad would have had a fit if they'd ever found out. They couldn't get their heads around the fact that Alice might possibly like a drink and behave like a normal teenager."

"But then it changed?"

"Radically. In her second year she started taking university, and herself, much more seriously." He stared up at the statue of Dionysus. "Ugly bugger, isn't he?"

"Your parents' choice of statue?"

Tim shook his head. "Ally's...well. He's Greek, isn't he?"

"The god of wine and winemakers. The Romans called him Bacchus."

"I don't think Ally gave a toss what the Romans called him. Greek mythology's her bag."

"'Mad as a box of frogs.' What did you mean by that?"

Tim smiled and didn't respond. "Mum said you and your friend are ghost hunters. Is that right?"

"Something like that."

"Cool, but I don't see how *that's* going to help you find her. My darling sister is very much alive."

"You know that for a fact?"

"I'd know if she wasn't," Tim said.

"You met Erik Strasser when he came to the house to try to get Alice to go with him, didn't you?"

Stephanie seemed to shudder at the question. After a long pause she nodded. "Yes, I met him."

"And what did you think of him?"

"Handsome, urbane and utterly charming. He tried to tell me that he was aware of Alice's problems and that he knew a doctor who could help her."

"But you didn't believe him?"

"Not at all. Oh, he was very persuasive, but—and I know this sounds a bit far-fetched—but I get a sense of people. I wouldn't go as far as Violet and claim I can see auras, but I can usually see through it when people are lying to me."

"And Alice? Does she have that kind of…what? Sixth sense?"

"I don't know. We've never discussed it. But I think not. If she had it, she would never have allowed herself to be taken in by him."

"I just thought he was a creep," George said. "He was still here when I came home from work. I called the police on him to get him to leave. I swear I was inches away from—"

"Yes, George you would have, what was it you said? Beaten him to a pulp?" Stephanie said, an edge of sarcasm in her voice. "I'm sorry. You're an accountant and you've never raised a finger in anger in your life. The most heated you get is if one of your clients is late with his tax returns."

George bridled, and then, realizing his wife knew him better than anybody, he reined in his indignation and sank back in his seat. "Well, I wanted to," he said. "That man took Alice away from us. My baby. I had such high hopes for her. Now I'm scared she'll end up in a gutter somewhere, one injection away from an overdose."

Harry leaned forward in his seat. "Let's try to be optimistic, shall we? I'm tasking my best people with finding out where Alice is. If she's with Strasser, we'll get her back for you—"

"And take her back to Mayberry?" Stephanie said hopefully. "Lawrence O'Connell said it was the best place for her."

"Yes, if that's what you want. I was there today. Richard Frost who runs the clinic seems very capable."

"Not capable enough to stop Alice walking out of there," George said bitterly.

Harry was going to say something about extenuating circumstances, but he didn't know what the Logans had been told, and he wasn't really ready to travel down that particular road just yet, not until he had a more solid grip on this case. He changed the subject. "I'd like a recent photograph of her, if you have one."

"George, where are those photos we took when we went to Rhodes last year?" Stephanie said. She turned to Harry. "Our last family holiday. We had a wonderful time."

"Was it Alice's idea, what with her interest in ancient Greece?'

"Good heavens no," George said. "A work colleague of mine has a villa out there. He lets it out when he's not using it. Not that Alice complained when I told her that was where we would be spending our summer break."

"She was thrilled to be going. Excited for weeks beforehand," Stephanie said.

"Those photos are on the computer," George said. "It won't take me long to find them and print one off for you."

"Full face," Harry said. "If you have one."

Chapter Eight

The girl was young and pretty, with cropped, dyed-black hair and kohl-lined panda eyes. She was a Goth, but then so were most of the people at the club, and Fin Clusky had dressed accordingly. "Can I get you a drink?" he said to the girl.

"Sure," she said. "Tia Maria and Coke." She leaned against the bar, next to him, leaning over and giving him a close-up view of a creamy cleavage enhanced by the purple bustier she wore.

He ordered her drink from the young barman dressed similarly to himself: skintight black jeans and a black tee-shirt, only Clusky's had an elaborate white skull and ivy leaf motif covering the front. "And mine's a Guinness," he said. He turned to the girl. "What's your name?" he asked her, leaning forward so he could hear her answer over the throbbing Evanescence track pounding from the club's speaker system.

"Kerry. What's yours? I've seen you here before."

"I'm Fin."

"Hello, Fin," she said and smiled. Clusky smiled back. He liked clubs like this—so easy to score.

Kerry moved well on the dance floor, losing herself in the sinuous music, her eyes partly closed, her lips mouthing the lyrics to the song. "I know where there's a party," Fin shouted in her ear.

"Where?"

"Close by. Coming?"

The girl stopped dancing. "Okay."

So easy, Clusky thought.

"Well?" Jason said as they headed back to the A1. "What did you make of them?"

Harry gripped the wheel, watching the road through the arcing of the wipers pushing aside the thin drizzle. "Average type of family," he said. "I wouldn't have believed she was Vi's sister if I didn't know that she was. So different."

"He was a bit of a wimp."

"Not really his fault. He's probably had all the fight knocked out of him." Harry flashed his lights at an oncoming car driving only on sidelights. "Idiot! They'll be pulling you out of a ditch one day," he yelled at the car as it passed.

"You seem wound up," Jason said.

"Yeah, I suppose I am. Just thinking about Alice and that bastard Strasser. The Logans might be a slightly dysfunctional family, but they don't deserve to be living through this kind of nightmare."

"And the boy? Tim?"

"Sick of living in his sister's shadow, I expect."

"Yeah, that's what I got."

"Sibling rivalry."

"Not that simple," Jason said. "I think he loves his sister, and he's probably as worried about her as the parents. Damned if he's going to show it though."

Harry smiled. "I remember being his age. Full of piss and vinegar, me against the world. I expect you were the same."

"I don't deny it. His sister's got a bee in her bonnet about ancient Greece, certainly. There's a statue of Dionysus in the garden. She chose it. Do you think Strasser might have used her interest in Greek mythology to lure her away?"

"That, or something like it. If I were the Logans, I'd be heartbroken, investing all that love and parental care, only to have it thrown back in my face. They're probably feeling as guilty as hell. Blaming themselves for letting their little girl slide off the rails."

"Do you think we can get her back?"

Harry shrugged. "I don't know, but I'm going to have a damned good try."

The street outside the club was almost empty. A lone taxi made its solitary journey from end to end, a black shark searching for a late-night punter. Clusky had his arm around Kerry as they stepped out into the night. She had drunk too many Tia Marias and was leaning against him for support. Fifty yards along, a dark blue van was parked, engine idling.

"How're we going to get there?" she said. "The party?"

"We'll fly, baby. All the way."

She didn't even feel the needle as it punctured her neck. As the chloral hydrate flooded through her bloodstream, she sagged against him. He tightened his hold around her waist to stop her falling to the ground. The blue van pulled away from the curb and traveled the fifty yards, braking in front of them. The doors opened and two young men climbed out. The first came across to Clusky and helped him support the girl. The second opened the van's side door. "Come on. Get her inside."

Before the taxi could make its second pass, Kerry, Clusky and the second man were in the back of the van and its door was pulled shut. The first man climbed in behind the wheel, gunned the gas pedal and sped off into the night. Less than thirty seconds had passed since Clusky had helped Kerry from the club. The empty taxi glided past the club. The driver had seen nothing. It was a slow night and he was bored.

Kerry flicked open her eyes. She was lying on something cold and hard. Her head was pounding and her mouth felt like it had been stuffed with cotton wool. She tried to turn her head to see where she was, but she couldn't move it. Something tight seemed to be clamping it rigid, and when she turned it, something sharp dug into her temples. She wanted to reach up to feel what it was, but she couldn't move her arms; they were strapped down at her sides. She swallowed, attempting to force saliva into her mouth. "Help," she managed to call, but it came out as little more than a croak.

A face loomed over her. "She's awake." It was Fin, the guy from the club.

"Whadyadoin?" she mumbled.

Another face appeared in her line of sight. Older, good-looking, staring down at her with a slight sneer. "She'll do. Let's begin."

She felt something—a knife—rip through the fabric of her bustier, and it came away, peeling back from her body, leaving her naked apart from a pair of black panties. Another two flicks of the knife and they too fell away from her. She opened her mouth to scream, but Fin was filling her vision again and he had the knife, jabbing it under her chin, the blade's point piercing the skin. "Not a sound or I'll cut you…badly."

Tears pricked out from Kerry's eyes and she began to softly whimper.

Harry dropped Jason off at Archway underground station and drove back to his flat in Maida Vale. He let himself in, picked up the mail lying on the doormat and carried on through to the lounge.

The light on his answering machine was flashing. He hit a button and a computerized female voice announced, "*You have two new messages. Message received today at 7.45 p.m.*" There was a bleep and Jane Talbot was talking to him.

"Hi, Harry. Sorry I missed you at the office, but it's been a hell of a day. I mentioned Erik Strasser to Rob, but he hasn't heard of him either. Sorry. See you in the morning."

"*Message two received today at 8.22 p.m.*" Beep. "Harry, it's Martin. Your Mr. Strasser is something of an enigma. I can track him back to 1998, but before that nothing. No birth or school records. It's as if he appeared on the German business scene fully formed. But it wasn't long before he started making a name for himself by buying up struggling software companies. In ten years he'd built himself quite a successful portfolio of different brands. He was so successful that he attracted the attention of the software giant Hematite. They bought him out in 2003 for a cool half a billion euros. They gave him the post of CEO until last year. I still can't get to the bottom of why he was ousted, but I have a contact in Dusseldorf who's looking into it for me. Check with me tomorrow and I'll tell you if we've uncovered anything else. Night." *"End of messages."*

Harry walked through to the kitchenette and switched on the kettle. A few minutes later he was sitting on his overstuffed armchair, shoes kicked off and a mug of Colombian in his hand. He switched on the small TV that sat on a battered Ikea bookcase, to watch the late-night news headlines. The newsreader had just launched into the first story when the telephone rang. He let the machine pick it up.

"Harry? It's Vi. Are you there? Are you still up?" He hauled himself off the couch and went to pick up the phone.

"Hello, Vi."

"Oh, you are there. I thought you would be. Stephanie just called me and told me you left her over an hour ago. How did it go?"

"Didn't she tell you?"

"She told me you were very kind and understanding, but didn't tell me much else."

"Well, there's not much else to tell really. I promised her I'd do everything I could to get Alice to go home. Nothing more to say."

"Well, I can tell you something that, perhaps, you don't know," Violet said.

"Fire away."

"Erik Strasser is not his real name."

Chapter Nine

"So, what's his real name, Vi?"

"Anton Markos. He isn't even German. He's—"

"Greek," Harry finished for her.

"Yes."

"That probably explains Alice's fascination for him. The girl's obsessed with the country. Ancient Greece, Greek mythology. He must have told her the truth about himself once he discovered her obsession. How did you find out?"

"I have a friend, Ellen, lives on the island of Kefalonia. She saw the picture on my blog page, recognized him and emailed me this evening."

"You have a blog page?"

"Don't sound so surprised. It's part of my network. How else do you think I get hold of this stuff? I lifted a picture from the Hematite Software online brochure and reposted it on my page, bracketed with question marks."

"Tell me more."

"He's the youngest son of the Markos family. They own large plantations of olive trees in the Chalcedon region in northern Greece. Made millions from the production of olive oil."

"How did your friend get to hear about him?"

"The family were hit by a sex scandal in the late nineties, a scandal that centered on the then twenty-year-old Anton. It was fairly big news at the time. It made the national press and TV. That was where Ellen remembered him from."

"Details?"

"Sketchy. She's going to dig out the relevant newspaper reports, scan them and email them through to me in the next few days. But, broadly, it involved the abduction and false imprisonment of several young women. Sound familiar?"

"Leopards and spots come to mind. So why isn't he languishing in some Greek jail?"

"As I said, the Markos family are wealthy, especially the father, Denes. Ellen believes Denes Markos paid out a small fortune to make the charges go away. Believe it or not, the rich can sometimes do that," she said with a cynical laugh. "Anyway, once all the fuss died down, Anton Markos disappeared from view, like he dropped off the planet."

"Only to resurface in Germany in 1998 as Erik Strasser," Harry said. "Any more, Vi?"

"Not just yet. I'll see what Ellen sends through to me and forward it on to you. Do you have an email address?"

"Don't be silly."

"Luddite. No matter. I pass everything on to Jason. He'll see you get it."

"Marvelous. Good night, Vi."

"Sleep well, Harry."

Kerry shivered.

She still didn't know where she was, but there was a draft blowing from somewhere and it was chilling her body and raising goose bumps on her skin. "Why are you doing this? What do you want from me?" she called out, but no one responded. Trying to move her head was too painful, and all she could do was to stare up at the ceiling, high above her.

There were lights hanging from the ceiling: industrial-looking lights with wide, white metal shades, each one holding a single bulb. She could see six from where she was lying, but she assumed there were more, because the bulbs were weak—she could stare directly at them without blinding herself—but the place she was being held in seemed quite well illuminated, so there had to be more than six. Just how big was this place?

She called out again, "Hey!" She still got no reply, but this time she heard the faint echo of her voice. The place had to be big. "Fin," she called. "Let me go, Fin. Untie me."

Away in the distance she heard voices, faint. They seemed to be in conversation, a soft susurration of sound, persistent but difficult to pin down. And then she heard footsteps and the occasional scrape of a shoe. Many feet walking over… what…concrete? In her mind's eye she could picture people entering the space, a crowd gathering. For what? To watch her? To watch her lying naked on what felt to her like a block of stone?

"Hey, help me!" she called again. And then she heard something that made her stomach feel hollow and brought the tears stinging back to her eyes. Someone laughed.

Harry finished his coffee and lay back in his seat, threading his hands behind his head and closing his eyes. He should go to bed, but the armchair was comfortable, and his mind was still thrumming from Martin's phone call.

It was unusual for Martin not to come up with anything new. He was very good at his job—the best in the country—and he'd had all day to work something up, but there was nothing, not even to corroborate the information in Violet's file. It bothered him. Maybe he'd be able to turn up more tomorrow.

He switched track and replayed the conversation with Violet in his head. Strasser was not German but Greek. Arrested on abduction and false imprisonment charges. Nothing more on his coven, nothing related to witchcraft at all. Something seemed wrong.

He trusted Violet Bulmer, trusted her instincts, but nothing he had seen or heard so far gelled with her insistence that Strasser/Markos was involved with something paranormal. He might be a pervert, might even be psychopathic, but that didn't make him a supernatural threat. There was the dead nurse and doctor, but nothing to say their deaths, coincidental as they were, were anything other than natural.

He had gone out on a limb in persuading Simon Crozier to involve the department, and, if he was honest with himself, he had traded on his and Crozier's longstanding friendship. Now he was beginning to think the limb he had stranded himself on was perilously thin—barely strong enough to support his weight, never mind the weight of a full Department 18 investigation.

He sat up abruptly and rubbed his eyes. "Damn it to hell, Vi, what have you gotten me into?" He stood up and stomped through to the bedroom.

Someone moved into Kerry's sight: the older man, tall and handsome, who was probably in his late thirties. Beside him a young woman, wearing a yellow silk blouse, blonde, almost white hair hanging straight down over her shoulders. She was looking straight ahead, her eyes glazed, not really registering what was happening.

Kerry stared her, her eyes pleading, but the girl seemed oblivious to her and continued to look ahead, her gaze fixed on a point Kerry couldn't see.

Kerry looked up again at the man. There was something about his eyes, and the way he seemed to regard her as something less than human, that escalated her fear and stopped her speaking. And then she saw a knife with a strange, odd-looking blade, long and gleaming, as he raised it above his head and brought it arcing down, plunging it into her chest, slicing into her aorta. The last thing she saw and heard was the blonde girl screaming, "No!" and then her vision dimmed and the world went black.

Harry awoke abruptly, flicked on the bedside lamp and checked his watch. Four o'clock. Shit! He really needed a good night's sleep, but, as was so often the case, the contrary alarm clock in his brain had kicked in. He lay there in the darkness, sleep just a memory and something he wouldn't revisit for another twenty or so hours.

At five thirty, with the sky beginning to lighten to a steely gray, he hauled himself from the bed and went through to the kitchen and ran himself a glass of water. He left the tap running, took the glassful in two long swallows, cupped his hand under the running water, splashed his face and turned on the television to watch the morning news.

He was still sitting, staring at the screen and not taking a word of it in, when Violet called him.

"It's six o'clock. Vi, what do you want?"

"I woke to find another email from Ellen, my friend in Kefalonia."

"I know who Ellen is."

"You sound tetchy."

"Bad night. What did the email say?"

"She managed to find a report about one of Anton Markos's victims."

"What did it say?"

"Not a lot, really. Stuff about how she was kept chained to a bed in a darkened room, how he got her hooked on heroin and fed her addiction daily, how she was so grateful when the police rescued her."

"So apart from the fact he's moved on from heroin to methamphetamine, how does this help us?"

"In essence, not a lot. But the article had a photo of the girl. Ellen scanned it and attached it to the email. Harry, I could be looking at a photograph of Alice."

"What do you mean?"

"Young, pretty, long blonde hair. It could be her twin sister. Don't you find it strange?"

Harry sighed. "Not really, Vi. All it displays is a preference. Pretty blondes obviously get his rocks off. It's quite common for a psychopath to target a type. They're usually a surrogate for the person the killer or abductor has in their own life—ex-wife or girlfriend, maybe even the mother."

"Elena Markos, Anton's mother, is a Mediterranean beauty—raven hair, olive skin, flashing brown eyes—and Markos was young, unmarried."

"An ex-lover then?"

"Reports suggest he was single and a virgin."

"Well, there's probably someone who fits Alice's and this other girl's description, locked away in his psyche somewhere."

"But it gives us an insight into his mind, and shows that Alice wasn't just some random target. He went after her specifically."

"I agree," Harry said. "I'm not sure it moves us any further forward in hunting him down."

Violet was silent for a few seconds, and then she said, "Harry, are you cooling on this?"

"No," he lied. "I said I'd help you find her, and I will. I just think we need to concentrate on Markos, or Erik Strasser, and not Alice's resemblance to one of his victims. It's just not significant enough."

Violet sniffed, her disappointment evident. "Ellen's going to track down his other victims. I wouldn't mind betting, here and now, they'll all be a similar type."

"You're probably right. I just wouldn't read too much into it. As I said, he might just have a thing for pretty blondes."

"Right, Harry, I'll be in touch."

He heard the phone slam down at the other end of the line.

"Great," he said sourly. "Now I've pissed her off." He switched off his phone, dropped it on the couch and went to take a long, hot shower.

Chapter Ten

Detective Inspector Susan Tyler picked her way carefully down the slime-covered stone steps. This part of the Thames riverbank was thick mud, and her boots squelched through it as she made her way across to the small group near the water's edge. Away to her right, a steady stream of commuter traffic made its laborious progress over Waterloo Bridge. A stiff breeze whipped her bobbed hair across her face, until she reached in her pocket for a black hair scrunchy and tied it back.

There were four people in the group. DC Brian Witherspoon, DS Jake Bartlett and a uniformed PC she didn't recognize, who looked like he should still be at school. The fourth member of the group was a woman in late middle age, with short silver hair and pointed features. Miriam Jackley was the police doctor on duty when the call came in of a body left stranded in the mud at low tide. She crouched over the naked body, examining it carefully and speaking her thoughts into a small digital recorder.

There were three other figures, dressed in white coveralls, examining the riverbank. Forensic. Another was standing to one side of the body, taking photographs.

"What have we got, Miriam?" Susan said as she reached them.

Miriam glanced up briefly and then went back to her examination. "Young woman, cause of death looks to be a single stab wound the chest."

Susan stared down at the body of a woman with short black hair, numerous facial piercings, tattoos on her arms and neck, with a reddish black hole through her left breast.

"How long has she been dead?" Susan asked, but didn't really expect an accurate answer.

"The body's cold," Miriam said. "But then it's been immersed in water. I would say for at least four hours, judging from the lividity of her skin tone. No damage from wildlife, so not that long."

Susan stared out at the muddy brown water "I wouldn't have thought wildlife would be that much of problem."

"You're kidding," Miriam said. "That might have been true a few decades back, but now the Thames is teeming with life. It's one of the least polluted metropolitan rivers in the world. Mitten crabs are my biggest problem. Voracious little buggers, they are. A floater like this is a banquet to them. And eels, they love a bit of dead meat."

Susan shuddered at the thought.

"But there's nothing on our lady here to suggest they had a go at her. All the marks on the body appear to be man-made. Ligature marks on the wrists and ankles, suggesting she's been restrained, and marks on either side of her head, at her temples, and this," she pointed to a red wheal across the young woman's brow, "that suggests her head was also restrained, possibly by some kind of strapping. We'll know more when the pathologist gets her to the lab. Ah, there he is." She nodded to a short, overweight, balding man making his way down the stone steps.

He waddled across to them. "Good morning, Miriam, Inspector Tyler. What have we got here?" Professor Duncan McBride looked down at the dead body and made a clicking noise with his tongue. "Oh dear. Poor girl. Your opinion, Miriam?"

"She's dead," Miriam said with a smile.

"Thanks for that insight," McBride said. "Very…er…insightful. What do you think killed her?"

"Apart from the hole in her chest, I really couldn't say. I'll leave that to you."

Susan was used to their banter and let them get on with it. She thought they secretly fancied each other and their apparent antagonism was a smokescreen. She turned to Witherspoon and Bartlett. "Who called it in?"

"He didn't leave a name, but the prat used his cell phone, so we're tracing him now."

"Well, you two get back to the station. I'll take it from here."

McBride was now hunched over the body, nearly head-to-head with Miriam. Susan could tell from their murmured asides that the banter was ongoing.

"Get a room, you two," she said. "Give me something I can use."

They both turned to look at her. "You can't rush science," McBride said. "I think Miriam and I are agreed, we'll know more after the postmortem."

"Great," Susan said.

"One thing," Miriam said. "I don't know what it signifies, but it might mean something to you. Someone has carved a small crescent shape in her lower abdomen, just above and to the side of the pubic bone."

"And she's had a two-pound coin in her mouth," McBride added. "Placed under her tongue."

"What?"

McBride beckoned her over. He had the girl's mouth open. Gently he lifted her tongue. "See?"

"Yeah," Susan said. She saw, but she didn't understand.

Jason tapped on Harry's open door and stepped into the office. "Morning."

"Good morning, Jason," Harry said, looking at him from over the top of the newspaper he was reading.

"I called in at Vi's on the way here. She asked me to give you this." He handed Harry a slim cardboard folder. Harry took it from him and laid it down on the desk.

"Aren't you going to open it?"

Harry drummed his fingers on the folder. "Soon."

"Vi said it's important," Jason said.

Harry continued drumming. "Soon," he said again. "How long have you known Vi, Jason?"

"About five years."

Harry nodded. "How does she seem to you?"

"What do you mean?"

"Is she behaving differently to the Vi you obviously know well?"

"Well, I think the last case we worked knocked the stuffing out of her."

"It was nasty," Harry said.

"And then some. We went in believing it was a residual haunting, which is just a playback of past events, no spirits involved, like pressing play on a DVD. Anne Boleyn in the Tower of London is a residual."

"I know what a residual is," Harry said. "I've encountered one or two in my time."

"Right. The family who lived in the house in Horringer reported seeing a man walking through a wall in their living room, carrying a scythe. Vi did the research and found that the site their house was built on back in the 1970s was once a farm, and she extrapolated from that, that what they were seeing was probably the echo of a farm worker who had met his death while going about his business. And the records bore that out. A worker at the Maddox farm had died when he'd fallen into a combine harvester back in the 1950s. So we went to the house to confirm this and to reassure the family that there was nothing to be concerned about."

"But Vi was wrong."

Jason nodded. "It wasn't a residual. It was an intelligent haunting. The spirit was very much real and knew we were there. It attacked us. I did a little digging when I came out of hospital, and it seems it was the spirit of Maddox himself. He'd discovered his wife was having an affair with one of the workers and killed them both with the scythe, buried his wife in one of his fields and threw the worker into the harvester, and then he hanged himself in the barn. All his rage was unleashed when Vi tried to get him to leave. I was badly beaten up, as was Vi, and she also sustained a slash across her back from the scythe that required fifty stitches. We were lucky to get out with our lives."

"So it must have affected her."

"Of course. She's been a paranormal investigator most of her adult life and never been injured before. But that wasn't it. The main reason she took it so badly was that she didn't research the haunting properly. And she blamed herself for my injuries. I was in hospital for six weeks, and she didn't visit me once. I don't think she could face me."

"And now?"

"We're back on track. It wasn't her fault. She was going on reports from the newspapers of the day. We went through them together and both agreed the haunting was harmless. I was as mistaken as she was and just as much to blame. I don't think she's quite back to one hundred per cent, but she's getting there. Why do you ask?"

Harry leaned back in his seat. "I'm not sure. There's something about this case that isn't hanging right. I can't quite make up my mind whether this stuff about Strasser is genuine, or whether Vi just wants us to find her niece."

"Do you think Vi would lie to you?"

Harry shook her head. "I wish I could answer that. I honestly don't know."

"Then we're going to continue this?"

"For the time being."

"So have you picked your team yet? Are you going to introduce us?"

Harry gave him a weary smile. "This is it. You and me. *We* are the team."

"Are you serious?"

"Until I know for certain that Strasser poses some kind of supernatural threat. If that proof comes through, I reevaluate the situation, but until that happens I'm afraid we're just going have to work this up ourselves."

"Vi won't like it."

"That's why we're not going to tell her," Harry said.

Chapter Eleven

Harry opened the folder Jason had given him and sat looking at a photocopied photograph of a young, pretty, blonde woman. Violet wasn't wrong. This could have been Alice's twin sister. There was a slight difference in the shape of the nose, but the resemblance was fairly close. He read through the news clippings, and offered the folder to Jason.

He shook his head. "I read it on the Tube. What do you make of it?"

"Strasser—or should we start calling him Markos?—sounds like a nasty piece of work, and I can understand Vi's desire to get Alice away from him." He lifted the picture from the folder. "And he obviously has a thing for blondes."

"So do I," Jason said. "But I don't go round abducting them and keeping them prisoner."

"May I remind you that Alice walked out of a secure clinic of her own free will and, as far as we know, went back to him? What does that tell us about her state of mind?"

"You met her parents. I should imagine she left to avoid suffocation."

Harry dropped the picture back on the desk. "Exactly. We could be dealing with nothing more than a case of teenage rebellion—a bit extreme, but all the *facts* in this case point to that."

The telephone on his desk buzzed twice. An internal call. He picked it up. "What can I do for you, Martin?"

"Strasser," Martin Impey said. "You asked me to dig. I have done. I've uncovered a few things you might find interesting."

"We'll be right down," Harry said, cradled the phone and turned to Jason.

"My researcher has a few facts about Strasser…sorry…Markos."

They took the elevator and five minutes later were sitting in Martin's office.

There were three desks in the office One of them, the biggest, was Martin's; the other two were occupied by his assistants. Martin introduced them to Jason. "Maggie and Christine, my right and left hands," he said.

Jason had been shown to a seat and was staring with admiration at the bank of computer screens covering one wall of the office. Each of the desks had wireless keyboards, a computer mouse and flat screen monitor. "I'm impressed with the tech," he said.

"Eyes and ears on the world," Martin said with a grin. "We were upgraded last month after years of waiting. We have some powerful servers in the room next door. It gives us access to worlds I could only have wet dreams about before."

"You're a geek," Jason said.

"And proud of it."

"Well you know what they say: 'The geek will inherit the earth'," Jason said.

Harry rolled his eyes. "Martin, what have you got for me?"

Martin switched his attention. "Yes, right. Well, for starters, Erik Strasser isn't really Erik Strasser. He's really—"

"Anton Markos," Harry finished for him and watched Martin's face fall.

"You knew? Do you how long it took us to discover that?"

"I only found out myself last night. Too late to call you and let you know."

"I suppose you know about his arrest in Greece and subsequent release?"

Harry nodded.

"How did you find out?"

"Vi Bulmer told me."

Martin let out an exasperated sigh. "Vi bloody Bulmer. I might have known. The department spends a couple of million on this computer setup, and Vi achieves the same results with what, a bloody telephone?"

"She has an extensive network of contacts," Harry said.

"And a very large and well-read library," Jason put in. "Plus the fact that her brain is a huge repository of arcane and obscure details."

"She's a bloody witch," Martin said with a smile. "Well, let's have all of it. What else did she tell you?"

As Harry filled him in, Jason struck up a conversation with Christine Buckley, the younger and prettier of Martin's assistants.

"Martin, do you have photos of all Markos's victims in Greece?" Harry asked.

Martin leaned over his desk and started hitting his keyboard. "Screen four, Harry. To your left."

Harry walked across to the bank of screens and stood in front of the fourth one along. A few seconds later the images of four young women appeared. All of an age. All pretty. All blonde. Anton Markos definitely had a preference. "Jason," he called. "Take a look at these."

Jason broke off his conversation with Christine and went across to where Harry was standing. "Over what period of time were these girls abducted?" Harry asked.

"Over a period of three years."

"And the police did nothing during that time?"

"From the reports I read, no. Three of the girls were released during that period. All admitted being with him, all said they had been with him voluntarily. All had developed an addiction to heroin."

"And the fourth girl?"

"She was still with him when they found her. Drugged out of her mind on crystal meth. He'd moved on from heroin by the time he took her. She wasn't so adamant that she was there by choice. It was her evidence that the police based their case on."

"Precarious."

"Very. It took three months of intensive digging into Markos and his life, during which time they located the first three girls. With their identical stories that they'd gone with him voluntarily, the police had nothing but the fourth girl's testimony. A week before the trial was due to start, the case fell apart. The fourth girl changed her story and said she'd been with him of her own free will. All the police could run with in the end was having sex with a minor. The legal age in Greece is fifteen. That girl there, the second one along, Alysia Carras, was only fourteen when Markos started having sex with her, so they proceeded to trial with that. But the case never reached the courtroom. It looks like palms were greased—pardon the pun—and the charges went away. Anton Markos was released and dropped off the face of the earth. At least, as far as I can ascertain."

"And then he resurfaces in Germany as Erik Strasser," Harry said.

"Indeed."

"Anything else? Vi tells me he's the high priest of a coven based here in the UK. Has she got her facts wrong?"

"Ah," Martin said. "Yes and no. He does lead a group of quasi-religious nuts, but I wouldn't describe it as a coven as such."

"What would you describe it as then?" Harry said. He was growing impatient. He wanted something, anything that would show Violet Bulmer was telling the truth.

"They call themselves the Children of Hecate. It's a cult who worship a Greek goddess of that name."

"So witchcraft yes or no?"

"Yes *and* no. Are they Satanists, no; are they Wiccan, again no. But Hecate is the goddess of witchcraft and sorcery, so yes. If you were painting the history of witchcraft on a very large canvas, they'd probably occupy a tiny spot in the bottom left-hand corner. I really know precious little about them, and despite all this," he swept an arm around the room, "so far, I've found out bugger all."

Susan Tyler walked into her office and picked up the ringing phone. "DI Tyler."

"Detective Inspector, it's Duncan McBride,"

"Hello, Professor," Susan said. She'd recognized the Scottish lilt to his voice before he introduced himself. "What can I do for you?"

"Could you pop along to the mortuary? I think I have something you're going to want to see."

"Concerning the body this morning?"

"Yes."

"Can't you tell me over the phone?"

"Yes, I could. But I think you'll want to see for yourself."

"I'll be there in thirty minutes."

The mortuary was situated in the basement of University College Hospital. Susan had been there a number of times before, but visiting the place still filled her with dread. She wasn't sure if it was the clinically spotless white tiles; the stainless steel tables, each with a drainage gulley; the sharp, antiseptic smell of the place; or maybe the banks of steel doors lining the walls, each a door to a refrigerated tomb. The presence of death freaked her out, and the experience of being here lived with her for days afterwards.

She pushed through the rubber entrance doors. McBride was there, his chubby form hovering by a stainless steel table. He was dressed in blue scrubs that barely contained his girth, his fluffy hair escaping from a blue scrub cap. Goggles were perched on his forehead and he wore latex gloves on his hands.

"Professor McBride," she said as she entered the room.

McBride's assistant was standing at a steel table holding another corpse, weighing something red on a set of scales that hung from the ceiling. Susan averted her eyes.

McBride turned to face her, his cheeks ruddy, his eyes large, magnified by the rimless spectacles he wore. In his hand was a long surgical knife, slightly curved. It glinted in the fierce overhead light. Duncan McBride looked like a slightly malevolent dwarf, a psychotic Doc from Disney's *Snow White*. "I'm sorry," he said in his soft Edinburgh burr. "I have a hectic schedule today, so I had to make a start. Come closer. You're not squeamish, are you?"

Susan took a breath. "No," she said. "I've seen dead bodies before. This isn't my first postmortem."

"That's right, it isn't," McBride said. "You came down for that really nasty rape and homicide last year. I remember now."

"What was it you wanted to show me?"

He stood aside, revealing the body of the girl they had recovered from the banks of the Thames. The only difference now was that she had a Y-shaped incision stretching from her pubis to her shoulders.

"I was just about to open her up. Want to watch? You'll have to gown up, of course."

"I'll pass. What was it you wanted to show me, Professor?"

He looked a little disappointed. "Shame. I rarely get an audience—apart from Phillip here. And he's seen it all before…many times. The novelty's worn off now, hasn't it, Phillip?" Phillip, his assistant, looked around at them, grimaced and carried on checking the scales.

"It's this," McBride said and pointed to the wound on the girl's breast. "What do you make of that? Look at the shape."

Susan leaned forward and looked at the wound.

"It's deep, about six inches," he said. "But the shape. Weirdest thing."

"It's a star," Susan said.

"Yes, a star. Made by a knife with five blades. Five blades somehow joined together to make one weapon. I took a photo of the wound." He walked across to the desk in the corner and came back clutching an eight-by-ten-inch color print. He handed it to Susan Tyler.

"When I first examined the body, I thought then that it had all the hallmarks of a ritual killing. The bound wrists and ankles, marks where the head was restrained, and now this."

It not only showed a blown-up image of the wound, but McBride had taken a pen and connected the points of the star. She looked at the shape he had formed by joining them.

"It's a pentagram," she said.

"Indeed it is. Are there any covens active in the area?"

"Not that I'm aware."

He looked disappointed again. "And then there's this." He pointed to a wound about three inches long, just above and to one side of the pubic bone—the crescent Miriam Jackley had pointed out to her at the riverside.

"Yes," she said. "Miriam showed me earlier."

"It was inflicted postmortem. The girl was dead when someone carved this into her. The shape of the stab wound, the crescent carving and the coin in the mouth indicate to me that there is an occult link to this. And you're not aware of a coven operating around here?"

"I've had nothing across my desk suggesting there is."

"And then there's this. A small stamp on the back of her hand." He lifted up the limp arm for Susan to see. On the back of the hand was a small, circular ink stamp.

"May I have a photo of this, and the wounds?"

"Of course," McBride said. "Phillip, fetch the camera."

Ten minutes later the photos were dropping into the printer's collection tray.

"I wanted to show you firsthand," McBride said, handing her the prints. "It might aid the investigation and help you find her killer."

"How old do you think she was?"

"Sixteen. No more. Could be younger. Tragic. I hope you catch whoever did this."

"Well, I'm going to try. Can I have a copy of your report?"

"Of course. I'll get it sent over as soon as it's typed up."

Susan went back to her car and drove back to the station. She was starting to get a bad feeling about this case.

Chapter Twelve

"Vi, have you heard of the Children of Hecate?" Harry said. "It's the name Markos's followers give to themselves."

"I've never heard that term used before." Violet sat in her library, a pile of books stacked on the desk in front of her. She was still wearing her dressing gown. She hadn't even showered yet. The email from her contact in Bremen had come in at seven, and since then she'd had her head buried in various textbooks and had been firing off emails to her contacts throughout the world. Personal hygiene had taken a backseat.

"How did you find out?" she said into the phone.

"Martin, here in the office. He and his girls were working on it all day yesterday, and again this morning."

"So you've stopped doubting me?"

"Vi, I never—"

"Harry, you know better than to flannel me. I knew from the outset that I hadn't convinced you, but I knew also that you would come round, once you'd dug a bit and discovered the facts for yourself."

"Martin was right. You *are* a witch."

"But a white one, Harry, not a black one. Never black."

"So we're moving forward. I was thinking of getting John McKinley to join the team."

"McKinley? Do I know him?"

"You met him once. African American, tall enough to play for the Harlem Globetrotters."

"Oh, John, yes. I remember. Charming man."

"And a powerful psychic. I think we might need him."

"I think you could be right. I got an email from my friend in Bremen. He's found out why Markos was removed as CEO at Hematite Software."

"Why"

"Wolfgang Metz, the chairman at Hematite, has a granddaughter, Karin. Markos started a relationship with her."

"Let me guess, a blue-eyed blonde?"

"On the money," Violet said.

"What is it with this guy and Nordic types?"

"I don't know. It seems to go deeper than just a penchant. He seems to be specifically targeting them. There's an underlying motive. So far I haven't discovered what it is, but I'll get there. Anyway, he zeroed in on Karin Metz, much to her grandfather's disapproval. They began a relationship, and old Wolfgang moved quickly to knock it on the head. Maybe he could see something in Markos that everyone else seemed to miss.

"Unfortunately Karin took his interference badly. She was totally in Markos's thrall, and her grandfather's actions started a family rift that still rumbles on to this day."

"What was the upshot?"

"Well, Wolfgang Metz is no fool. With some shrewd boardroom maneuvering, he had Markos removed as CEO, effectively putting him out of work. He also has some powerful friends and he called in some favors. The police got involved at the highest level, and a judge slapped a restraining order on Markos that stopped him having any contact with Karin. Markos was now in a corner. Thanks to Wolfgang, he was unemployable in Germany and he couldn't have contact with Karin. So he left and came to England to start again."

"I see a pattern emerging here. Flee, rather than face the consequences of his actions."

"Exactly. And he carries on where he left off. Going by his past history, his involvement with Alice has nothing to do with romance, or, if it has, it's from her side only. To him she's just a cipher. She could be any pretty blonde. I think the man's sick."

"Well, he obviously has issues," Harry said. "How does all this tie in with the Children of Hecate?"

"I don't know. But I think if we keep examining Anton Markos, we're going to find out. I'm glad you're bringing John McKinley in. He can help you here in London. I think Jason can be useful elsewhere."

"Really? Where?"

"Austria. Karin Metz's family shipped her off there to get over the affair with Markos. She now works as a ski instructor in Kitzbühel. Send Jason over there. Get him to use his charm on her. I know Jason's strengths. He can charm the birds off the trees. See what he can get her to spill about Markos. It may be our chance to finally get an advantage over him."

"Do you think Jason will agree to go?"

"He'll agree, and I should think he'll love every minute of it."

"Can you ski?" Harry said when Jason entered the office.

"Yes, why?"

"Because you're going on a trip. How does an all expenses paid holiday to Austria sound?"

"What's the catch?" Jason asked suspiciously.

"You're going to have to form a relationship with a beautiful young blonde and pump her for information about Anton Markos."

"Sometimes this job sucks," Jason said with a smile.

Susan walked into the incident room and across to the board affixed to the wall. The board was empty apart from a photo in the center, taken on the riverbank. The room was half-full. Witherspoon and Bartlett were there along with two detective constables, one male, one female. The male DC, Tom Fox, was three years out of Hendon and was climbing rapidly up the promotion ladder. He was expected to reach the rank of sergeant before he hit twenty-five. Gillian Ryder had already reached twenty-five but was still a DC and showed no great ambition to climb higher.

"What have you got for me?" Susan said.

"We have a name for the victim," Gillian said. "Kerry Green, sixteen, from Hackney. She was already in the system, a couple of juvies and a shoplifting charge last year that resulted in her being printed."

"We've also identified the caller," Fox said. "His name is Arthur Lane."

"Do we like him for this?" Susan said.

"I went to interview him first thing. He's seventy-two, a retired postal worker from Penge. He saw Kerry's body and called it in."

"Why didn't he leave a name?"

"The usual," Fox said. "Didn't want to get involved."

"So if he lives in Penge, how did he get to see the body?"

"He's been staying with his sister in Belvedere Road. He was walking her dog along the Embankment."

"So we have no lines of inquiry so far."

There was a general shaking of heads around the room.

"Well, I've just got back from a meeting with McBride at UCH. There were a few marks on the body he wanted me to see." She opened her briefcase and took out three color prints. She pinned them to the wallboard and stood back. "Okay. Image one: the stab wound, and probably this is what killed her. Notice the shape of the puncture wound."

"It's a star," from the room.

"Professor McBride believes it was made by a five-bladed knife."

"Odd."

"Yes, that's what he thought. He thinks it's five blades welded together along the blunt edges, contained in a single handle. He thinks it might be ceremonial in some way. As you see, it leaves a star-shaped wound. I don't know how significant this is, but if you join the points of the star together, they form a pentagram, an occult symbol. So we need to look at any groups in the area with some kind of black magic connection. Check with local cemeteries—see if they've had any incidents of graves being interfered with, headstones defaced, statuary vandalized, that kind of thing. Also check with the library and local bookshops to see if they've been asked for any books on the subject."

"What about the Spiritualist church in Cooper Street?"

"No, we won't go after the Christians just yet. Let's concentrate our efforts on the fruit loops and oddballs." She turned her attention back to the board. "The second photo. Someone carved this into Kerry's flesh, postmortem according to McBride. Again the symbol suggests some kind of occult connection. It's a crescent and could signify a new moon. And finally this, the remains of an ink stamp on the back of her hand."

"That's a nightclub reentry stamp," Gillian said.

"Reentry?" Susan queried.

"Antismoking laws. If you're at a club and you want to go outside for a cigarette, they stamp the back of your hand so you can go back inside without having to pay again."

"Yeah, I've heard of that. Right, Gill, make copies of the photo and get uniforms to canvass the clubs in the area. See if anyone can identify it. And that is all, for the time being. We need to tell Kerry Green's parents and get them over to UCH to identify the body."

"I'm on it," Witherspoon said.

"And while you're at it, have a word with them, gently, to see if they knew of any involvement their daughter had with any cults or groups. You never know; we might strike it lucky. But, I emphasize, *gently*. Kid gloves."

Susan went back to her office and picked up the phone. She took a crumpled card from her top pocket and dialed.

"Harry Bailey?"

"Mr. Bailey. I don't know if you remember me. Detective Inspector Tyler, Waterloo Road CID."

"Inspector, yes. Of course I remember you."

"How's your boss, Mr. Crozier, after his stabbing?"

"He's made a full recovery, thank you."

Two years ago Simon Crozier had been attacked, stabbed by a woman with a kitchen knife, walking home along the Embankment. DI Susan Tyler had been the SIO on the case.

"What can I do for you, Inspector?"

"I need your help with a case I'm currently investigating."

"Sure," Harry said. "Anything I can do to help."

"Last night a young girl, Kerry Green, was murdered. A single stab wound to the heart."

"And?" Harry said. "How would that concern Department 18?"

"We have reason to believe it could be some kind of ritual killing. From the investigation of your boss's attack, I discovered that your department deals with the weird and the wonderful, so I thought we might share a mutual interest. Can you come down here so we can talk?"

"No," Harry said. "But you are welcome to come here. You remember where we are?"

"I do. Thirty minutes?"

Susan walked back to the incident room. Jake Bartlett was standing, staring at the photographs on the board.

"Jake, I have to go out for an hour or two. You can get me on my cell."

"Nasty," Bartlett said, pointing to the photo of Kerry on the riverbank. "She was only a kid. Sixteen. My Casey's age. We'll get the bastard who did this."

"Yes, Jake." Susan squeezed his arm. "We'll get him."

"Right, you're on a flight out of Gatwick at 17.50 to Munich, and a taxi's booked to take you to Kitzbühel. You're staying at the Hotel Jägerwirt, bed and breakfast. You can organize your own evening meals. There are some very nice restaurants in the town. It will give you a chance to find somewhere classy to take her to dinner. The ski school is affiliated to the Jägerwirt, so you should cross paths with her without much effort."

"How will I know her?"

Harry slid a photograph across the desk. Jason spun it around to see it.

"Yowza!"

"Yowza? What are you, fourteen?"

"She's hot."

"She's also damaged goods. She narrowly escaped Markos's clutches, but while she was with him she was totally infatuated. We don't know her current state of mind, so tread lightly. Remember, her family is very wealthy, very protective and very powerful. You'll probably be vetted in some way minutes after making contact with her. Don't give them any cause for concern. We want information. We don't want to drive her to a breakdown. Okay?"

"I hear you. Well, I should go home and pack. How long is the hotel booked for?"

"You're booked in for three nights. It would be nice if you could get some results sooner."

"I'll do what I can."

As Jason walked out of the office, he passed an attractive woman in the corridor, possibly mid forties with neatly bobbed, light brown hair. She was wearing a dark blue business suit. "Harry Bailey?" she said.

"Keep walking. The door at the end."

Susan thanked him, reached the door and knocked.

"Come in."

She pushed open the door and stepped inside.

Harry was on his feet and walking around the desk to greet her as she stepped into the room. "Inspector Tyler," he said. "A pleasant surprise to hear from you. Here, take a seat." He guided her to an office chair opposite his, and went back to the other side of the desk and sat down. "Now, how can we help you? You said something about a murdered girl?"

Chapter Thirteen

"Her name was Kerry Green, sixteen, found on the banks of the Thames, just down river from Waterloo Bridge. We believe she was killed sometime last night and her body dumped in the river."

Harry stared down at the photo in front of him. It showed a naked girl with cropped black hair and several piercings. She had a stab wound in her chest.

"Just a kid," he said, almost to himself. He'd been expecting to see the body of a pretty young blonde. This surprised him. It probably had nothing to do with Markos.

"Look at the wrists, ankles and forehead. The marks suggest she'd been restrained at some point in the twelve or so hours leading to her death. The nature of the stab wound and the carving on the torso, coupled with the restraint marks, leads us believe that this was some kind of ritual killing, perhaps a ceremony gone wrong…or right, depending on your viewpoint. We were wondering if you were aware of any satanic cults or covens operating in the area?"

"Well, I can think of one off the top of my head. They call themselves the Children of Hecate."

"Devil worshipers? Satanists?"

"Well, they're certainly something, though what their particular craziness is, I haven't been able to find out yet. Would you like a coffee?"

"Yes, I would."

Harry reached out and pressed the button on the intercom on his desk. "Melanie, two coffees, please. One black, no sugar…" He looked across at Susan, a question in his eyes.

"White. One sugar," she said.

Harry repeated the request into the intercom.

"What else can you tell me about...what was it? The Children of Machete?"

"*Hecate*," Harry corrected her. "The Children of Hecate. Well, not a great deal really. We've only just started investigating them."

"For what reason?"

"It's what we do," Harry said. He didn't want to give her a complete answer. At least, not yet. "They seem to be governed by a man called Erik Strasser, real name Anton Markos, a Greek national with a shady past. He has a penthouse apartment in Clerkenwell, a house in the country, and he owns a warehouse somewhere in Docklands, where I believe his group hold their meetings."

"Do you know where in Docklands?"

"Haven't a clue. As I said, we only started the investigation yesterday. Details are still a little sketchy."

The door opened and Melanie Cole, Harry's secretary, came in with the coffee. She set the tray down on the desk and retreated to the outer office.

"Well," Harry said, taking his mug from the tray. "How's the world of law enforcement?"

"Why were the police here?" Simon Crozier said.

Harry sat across the desk from him. Crozier had eyes everywhere. It was hard to get anything past him. "DI Susan Tyler," Harry said. "She was the senior investigating officer when you were attacked. She wanted some help with a murder case she's running. I think it might have a connection to ours."

"What, the Strasser case?"

"It's the Markos case now," Harry said. "Anton Markos is Erik Strasser's real name."

"And have you swapped information?"

"Some," Harry said.

"Why? We try not to use the boys in blue in our inquiries."

"I think it might be useful. We're searching for Anton Markos. We can use the Met's manpower to track him down. It will save us money in the long run."

Simon Crozier stared at him thoughtfully. "Well, I suppose it *will* offset the cost of a three-night, all-expenses trip to Austria," he said. "Why did you send someone to Austria?"

"To meet someone who had direct involvement with Markos."

"Who did you send?"

"Jason West."

"Vi Bulmer's assistant?"

"He's helping us."

"So are the world and his wife, apparently. What happened to the time when we handled everything in-house?"

"Times change, Simon."

"But why West? He's had very little experience."

"He has a specialized talent," Harry said.

"Really? What is it?"

"He can ski."

"So can I."

"Maybe, but Jason's thirty years your junior, and he has an eye for the ladies...which kind of rules you out."

Crozier smiled. "Fair play, Harry. I trust your judgment."

"And Susan Tyler?"

"I agree with you. We can use the Met's resources. Go and see her again. Show her everything you have on the Markos case. If the police can track him down, it's going to save us an awful lot of legwork."

"No limits?"

"Use your discretion, Harry. Stay away from the more controversial of the department's methods."

"Fine," Harry said. "I'll go and see her. Do you want me to walk you through what we've got so far?"

Crozier settled back in his seat. "Why not?" he said. "It won't do me any harm to hear how you're spending the department's money."

From Crozier's office, Harry took the elevator down to the second floor to pay John McKinley a visit.

"Have you got much on at the moment, John?"

John McKinley sat behind his desk, long legs crossed, reading a paperback novel. "At the moment the department is paying me to sit here and read thrillers. What can I do for you, Harry?"

Harry pulled up a chair and for the third time that day found himself going through the Anton Markos case. The more he revisited it, the more necessary he found his and Department 18's involvement to be.

McKinley sat and listened patiently. When Harry had finished, he stood up and walked to the window. "How long have you known Violet Bulmer?" he said.

"Over twenty years," Harry said.

"And you trust her account of what's going on?"

"I've come to believe it."

"But you doubted her before."

"I was in two minds," Harry said honestly. "But the more I hear, the more I think he's a viable threat."

"Then count me in."

"Just like that?"

"I'm running out of books to read," McKinley said. "Unless I keep my hand in, I'm going to vegetate. So, I'll do anything I can to help. How old are the girls he's targeting?"

"Teenagers mostly."

"The question you have to ask yourself is why? Are they just surrogates for the one he really wants?"

"That thought crossed my mind. It's possible we'll know more when Jason reports back from Austria."

"I'm relieved I didn't get that gig. Britain's climate is cold enough for me.

I don't think I could handle Austria—months of snow and temperatures of minus twenty. I'm like a cat, Harry. I need warmth. Sometimes I really crave the California sunshine."

"Lightweight," Harry said.

"And I make no apologies for it. Can I see all the relevant files?"

"I'll get Melanie to make copies and run them down to you."

McKinley picked up his book again. "Only three chapters to go. I'd better get it finished. I might not get the chance in the coming days."

"I appreciate it, John."

"I know, Harry. What are friends for?"

"Welcome to the Hotel Jägerwirt, Mr. West. Have you visited Austria before?"

The woman behind the desk was in her forties. She was wearing a flared gray skirt, a bright red blouse and a colorful embroidered waistcoat—Austrian national dress. Her fair hair was parted in the center and plaited, the plaits wound in coils and pinned to cover her ears. To Jason it was if she'd stepped through some kind of time warp and come here from the nineteenth century.

But she was very polite and her English was impeccable. "You are in room 302. If you leave your bag here, I'll have Franz, our porter, bring it up for you."

"It's okay, I can manage."

"As you wish." She handed him a key on a large plastic fob bearing an image of the hotel. A five-story, chalet-style building with picturesque window boxes filled with vermillion pelargonium. The hotel was large but still maintained an old-world charm.

"But, one thing. I'd like to book a skiing lesson for tomorrow morning."

"That won't be a problem." She took out a large appointment book from under the desk and opened it out flat in front of her. "Would you describe yourself as a novice, intermediate or advanced?"

"Intermediate, I suppose. I've skied since childhood, but never tackled a black run."

"Well, they're for expert, accomplished skiers."

"I'm somewhere between blue and red. I suppose I'm looking for someone who can give me a refresher course. I haven't skied in over five years."

She stared down at the book and tapped her pen against her teeth. "I'm thinking Dieter. He's very good."

"A friend of mine got back from Austria last week. He had a very good instructor, a young woman. Karin...Katz?"

"Metz. Karin Metz. She takes novices through to advanced. She's excellent." She consulted the book again. "And you're in luck. She has a window from eleven through to one o'clock. Would that be suitable?"

Jason gave her a warm smile. "Ideal. I can get into town and hire boots and skis. I didn't bring any with me."

The receptionist regarded his solitary suitcase. "Yes, I can see that. There's a shop on Josef Herold-Strasse. They should be able to provide you with everything you need." She slid one of the store's advertising fliers across to him.

He folded it and slipped it into his pocket. "And I wondered if I could book a table in the restaurant for this evening."

She tapped a few keys on the laptop on the desk. "It's very early in the season. We're only one-third full. You can come down for a meal anytime up until nine o'clock."

"Fantastic. You've been really helpful."

The woman smiled and inclined her head. "You're very welcome. Enjoy your stay, Mr. West."

"Brian, have you spoken with Kerry Green's parents yet?" Susan said as she came back into the interview room.

"I tried. They were out. I'm going back shortly."

"Wait for me. I'll come with you."

"We've had a result on the stamp," Gillian said. "It matches one they use at the Abyss in Soho."

"Good."

"Do we go and check it out?"

"Not just yet. I'll see if I can get a recent picture of Kerry from her parents. We'll go to the club then and show it around. See if anyone recognizes her. Brian, you ready?"

Brian Witherspoon pulled his jacket from the back of a chair and put it on. "Shall I drive?"

"What do you think?" Susan said.

Chapter Fourteen

Susan knocked on the canary-yellow front door on the first floor of Clarkson House, a high-rise, part of a sink estate on the Hackney/Stamford Hill border.

Witherspoon looked out nervously from the window at his car, vulnerable in a parking space outside.

"If I come back and my wheels have been taken, I'm claiming compensation."

Susan ignored him and rapped on the door again. As the door opened, the smell of marijuana smoke wafted out at her. "Linda Green?" she said to the slatternly woman standing in the doorway, regarding her with a hostile stare.

"Who wants to know?"

Susan produced her warrant card and held it out for the woman to see. "Detective Inspector Tyler. This is Detective Constable Witherspoon. We're from Waterloo Road police station."

"A bit far off your patch, aren't you?"

"Who is it, Lin?" a male voice drifted out.

"Police," she called back.

"Shit!" the voice said, followed by the sound of running feet and a toilet flushing. "What do they want?"

"What do you want?"

"It's about your daughter, Kerry."

"What's the silly little bitch done this time?"

"I'm afraid I have some very bad news, Mrs. Green. I'm sorry to say your daughter is dead."

Linda Green looked at her, the hostile look replaced by one of incredulity.

"Dead? Kerry?"

"I'm very sorry," Susan said. "My sincerest condolences. May we come in?"

"Dead?" Linda said. The blood had drained from her face, and she clutched the doorframe to support herself as she sagged against it. "Yes," she said. "Come in." She moved to one side to allow them into the flat.

"What's going on, Lin?" A man wearing a stained vest and a bellicose expression lurched out of a room to the left. "You let them in?" he said. "You let the filth into the flat?"

"It's Kerry, Pete. She's dead."

"Dead? What do you mean, dead?"

"We're sorry, Mr. Green. Kerry was found—"

"He's not my husband. Kerry's father walked out on us ten years ago. Lives with some whore up in Grimsby. Pete's my boyfriend. Pete Roberts. Come through." She led the way through to an untidy lounge. A large plasma TV sat in the corner of the room. There was a football match playing at full volume.

"May we turn that off?" Susan said, pointing to it.

"But it's Arsenal, they're playing Tottenham," Roberts said and made no move.

"Turn the fucking box off, Pete. Kerry's dead!"

"But they're losing."

"Then go down the pub and watch it there. Drown your sorrows at the same time. Drown yourself while you're at it," she added under her breath.

Roberts snatched his jacket from the back of the settee and threw it on. Grumbling, he pushed past them. A second later the front door slammed.

"Him and Kerry don't get on," Linda said, as if that excused his ignorant behavior. And then she turned off the TV, went and sat down heavily on the settee. "What was it? Drugs?"

"May we sit?"

Linda nodded and waved them to the armchairs.

"We have reason to believe your daughter was murdered. We'd like you to come and formally identify the body?"

"You mean you don't know for certain it's her?"

"We're pretty sure, Mrs. Green. Kerry was fingerprinted last year during her arrest for shoplifting. The prints match those taken from the scene. When did you last see Kerry?"

"Last night. She was going uptown. A club, I think."

"The Abyss?"

"If you say so. Once she walks out of that door, she does what she pleases. She's sixteen."

"Do you have a recent photo of her?"

"Murdered, you say? Who the hell would want to kill Kerry? She can be a pain in the ass at times and she dresses like a freak. But murdered? Who killed her?"

"That's why we need your help, to try and find her killer."

Linda was swaying in her seat and blinking furiously, as if she was trying to understand why a bomb had just exploded in her life.

"The photo?" Susan said, pressing her.

"I've got one. Taken at school last year. Will that do?"

"May we see?" Witherspoon said.

"Hold on." Linda got to her feet and went across to a seventies-style teak sideboard. She pulled out a drawer and started to rummage through it. After a few moments she produced a cellophane envelope. "Here they are." She ripped the seal from the envelope and took out a five by seven glossy color picture of a pretty girl with mousy hair and glasses, braces on her teeth. She handed it across to Witherspoon, who looked at it. "And this is Kerry?"

"Yes. She was pretty before she got into all that emo stuff. Cut all her hair off and dyed it black. Started getting all those awful piercings. Not hygienic, those things. 'You'll get AIDS', I told her, but did she listen?"

"Have you got a photo of Kerry looking like that?" Witherspoon asked.

"I think so." Linda went back to the drawer and start looking again. Finally she said, "Taken at a family party last month," and handed it across. "Though what you want that one for? She looks bloody awful."

Witherspoon stared at the picture. The pretty girl had gone. This one looked more like the girl they had found dead on the banks of the Thames. He handed the photo to his DI.

Susan took it and put it in her pocket. "We'll let you have this back."

"Keep it," Linda said. "That's not my daughter." She lifted the school photo. "*That's* my Kerry," she said and started to cry.

"Apart from the Goth scene she was involved in, did Kerry mention any groups or cults she had contact with?"

Linda shook her head. "No, nothing like that." She blew her nose loudly into a tissue.

"Is there someone you can call, to be with you?" Susan asked.

"Mum lives two doors down. I'll call her."

"Also," Susan said. "Were you and your…boyfriend here last night?"

"DVD and curry night," Linda said distractedly and blew her nose again.

"And you were here all night. Someone can verify that?"

Linda fixed them with another hostile look. "You think I killed my own daughter?" she said.

"We have to ask, Mrs. Green. To eliminate you from our inquiries."

"My mum was here with us. It was curry night. She never misses it. Ask her. She lives two doors down. Number twenty-one."

Susan got to her feet. "Well, that will be all, Mrs. Green. I'll send a car for you tomorrow to take you to the mortuary. Nine o'clock."

Linda didn't respond. She sniffed into the tissue again and waved them away.

"We'll see ourselves out," Witherspoon said, and followed his boss to the door.

Once outside in the hallway, he said, "Are we going to check the mother?"

Susan shook her head. "No. She wasn't lying. We know where they are if we need to interview them again. Check on the boyfriend though. Pete…"

"Roberts? You think he might be involved?"

"He seemed more upset that Arsenal were losing than about Kerry. See if he's got form. Come on, let's head back."

"Unless my wheels have been stolen," Witherspoon said.

Susan got back to Waterloo Road police station to find Harry waiting for her. "What can I do for you, Mr. Bailey?" she said as she walked through the swing doors.

"Call me Harry, please, if we're going to be working together."

"*Are* we going to be working together?" she said, sweeping past him.

"I certainly think we can help each other out."

She stopped and glanced back at him. "Come through to my office," she said.

She led him though a network of corridors until they came to an office he had been in before. He dropped the file he was carrying down on Susan Tyler's modern-looking dark blue desk. She walked around the desk, sat down and said, "What's this?"

"Everything we have on Anton Markos and the Children of Hecate."

She opened the file and started leafing through the contents. Finally she looked up at him. "Why are you showing me this now?"

"In the interests of interbureau cooperation," she said.

"Bollocks," she said. "You want to use the Met's resources to help you with your investigation."

Harry smiled. "We all work for the same boss," he said.

"The difference being that your office is three times the size of mine and your desk is oak instead of melamine-covered chipboard."

"Agreed, but we have a lot we can bring to the party."

She stood up abruptly. "I'll see if I can rustle up a cup of coffee; then we'll talk." She left the room, returning a few seconds later. "It's on its way. Black, no sugar, right?"

"Well remembered."

She went back to the file. After a few moments she said, "All very interesting, but it gives us nothing new we can use."

"I'm showing you the file to give you a clearer picture of who we're dealing with."

She took an electronic cigarette from her purse, stuck it between her lips and let the nicotine vapor spill into the air. "Ironic really," she said. "I started using this to help me quit smoking. I no longer smoke, but I'm hooked on this bloody thing." She tapped the file. "The methamphetamine he got your friend's niece hooked on, he would need a steady supply of it. We can target known dealers, see if we can get some kind of lead there." She picked up the photo of Markos leaving the restaurant in the West End. "Good-looking sod, isn't he?"

"You can see why he attracts these girls."

"A handsome face and a whiff of money. Quite a devastating combination. Have you got an address for his place in Clerkenwell?"

"Goswell Road. He has a penthouse apartment with a view of St Paul's, apparently."

"And his place in the Cotswolds?"

"A seventeenth-century manor house in Fairford, overlooking the River Coin. Both addresses are in the file. Last page."

She flicked to the final page and scribbled both addresses on her desk blotter. "But nothing on this supposed warehouse in Docklands where he and his followers meet?"

"I have my best people working on it. We'll have an address soon."

"It still leaves us with the problem that we have nothing concrete to justify a search warrant for any of his places." She took the photograph of Kerry Green from her bag and handed it to Harry. "*She* doesn't fit into the blue-eyed blonde category."

Harry stared at the photograph. "And this is the girl you found dead by the Thames."

Susan nodded.

"So how does she fit into all this...unless..."

"What?"

"She's the only dead one."

"So what does that mean?"

"Perhaps the girls have different purposes. You said the pathologist thought the killing of this girl was ritualistic."

"Judging from the marks on the body. And she had a two-pound coin under the tongue."

"To pay the ferryman, Charon, to carry the body across the river Styx to the afterlife."

"So what do we do? Arrest Chris de Burgh?"

Harry smiled. "No. What I'm saying is that she could have been a sacrifice. Maybe the blondes are serving a different purpose."

"What?"

"I don't know. I might have more idea when I hear back from Jason."

"Who's Jason?"

"Jason West, he's working for me. I've sent him to Austria to meet one of Markos's former lovers. Karin Metz, a German girl. Blonde, blue eyes, like the others. Maybe we can get a handle on Markos's motivation by talking to her."

"What do we do in the meantime?"

"Keep digging, I suppose. Have you tracked down Kerry Green's movements for last night?"

"We're working on it. We think she went to a club, the Abyss in Soho. We'll go there tomorrow evening. We'll take the photo and show it around. If she met with her killer, someone might have seen her. We might even get a name? You never know."

"You can't go there before."

"It won't be open until the evening."

Harry tutted. "Frustrating. The wheels of justice grind inexorably slowly."

Susan raised her eyes to the ceiling. "Tell me about it."

"I suggest we stay in close contact. If either of us turns up anything significant, we'll let the other know. Agreed?"

"What the hell, yes. What have we got to lose?"

"Nothing. But we might have everything to gain."

Chapter Fifteen

Clusky sat at the bar in the Abyss, nursing a half-drunk pint of Guinness. He was still buzzing from the thrill of last night—watching the girl die and disposing of her body, seeing it fall into the water from Waterloo Bridge.

At three fifteen in the morning, there had been no traffic on the bridge: no cars, no pedestrians. It had been an easy matter to haul her from the trunk of the car and drop her into the Thames. Traffic cameras might have recorded the incident, but Fin didn't care. They would never recognize him, never see past the hoodie and the mask he was wearing. And the car he was driving, he'd stolen earlier in the evening. He was fireproof and was reveling in his anonymity.

He was enjoying his connection to Erik and the Children of Hecate. Not that he believed any of that occult mumbo jumbo. But he enjoyed hunting for targets and the resulting sacrifices, and especially enjoyed being given the bodies to get rid of. There had been three so far, Kerry being the best. She'd still been warm when he loaded her body into his car. Warm and dead. Just how he liked them. Dead girls never complained, no matter what he did to them.

"Hey, Fin. How's it going?"

The familiar voice broke him from his reverie. The voice belonged to Terry Butler. The last thing Clusky needed right now was Butler's drunken intrusion into his own private contemplations.

"When are you going to take us back to that gaff in Clerkenwell? Christ, that was a night. That girl, Alice, on the balcony. Stupid bitch. Man, was she out of it. Are they still together, that girl and Strasser?"

Clusky shrugged. "I dunno. Never see them now."

"Why not? Man, I thought you were set up for life there. How much ice did you supply him?"

"Keep your voice down," Clusky hissed, and moved towards him threateningly.

"Hey, keep calm, man. I didn't mean anything by it. That was a great night though. Shame Davy decided to dance with a train, but he was *so* stoned. I wasn't surprised when I heard. You seen Mikey?"

"No, I haven't seen Mikey. I told you both then, you thick, English prick, don't contact me till I tell you otherwise. So fuck off," Clusky said.

"Hey, what's up with you, man?" Butler slurred. "You pissed off with me or something? What have I done wrong?"

"I'm busy," Clusky said.

Butler looked from side to side, to see what Clusky was busy with, but saw nothing. "You carrying? I've got money. I can pay."

The knife appeared in Clusky's hand as if by magic. He kept it low, but jabbed it at Butler's side. "I said, fuck off, and I meant it."

"Hey," Butler said quietly. "Lighten up, man. I get it. You want to be alone. I'm going. Jesus!"

As Butler moved away, Clusky closed the knife and slipped it back into the pocket of his jeans. Moments later his mind was trying to get back in the car with Kerry, and she was going to do whatever he wanted. But he couldn't get there—couldn't sustain the mood. Butler had ruined it.

He slammed his hand down on the bar, making the glasses jump, swallowed the last of his pint and left the club. He walked back to the side street where he'd left his Suzuki motorcycle, slipped on his crash helmet, mounted the bike and started the engine. Seconds later he was riding across London, heading east.

The alarm woke her at six. After a cereal bar and an energy drink, Susan dressed and walked down to the Embankment. At the point where they recovered Kerry Green's body, she stopped and stared down at the water as it flowed sluggishly towards Greenwich. She looked back at Waterloo Bridge thoughtfully, took out her cell phone and dialed the station.

Gillian answered on the second ring.

"Gill, anyone else in yet?"

"DS Bartlett, but he's in the canteen getting breakfast. Do you want him?"

"No, you can do it. Get on to Traffic. I want them to review the footage from the traffic cams on Waterloo Bridge, both directions."

"Okay. What time frame?"

"Let's say midnight through to five a.m."

"They're going to love that."

"I don't care. Just get them to do it. See if they have footage of any unusual activity."

"Like?"

"Like someone throwing Kerry Green's body off the bridge."

"I'm on it," Gillian said.

"Great. I'll be in soon." Susan rang off.

Harry sat in his lounge, watching breakfast TV. He'd been watching news programs since five. Now it was the usual daytime fare of celebrity interviews, glib reports of things that were happening in the world, and competitions where viewers could win a year's salary and a brand-new car by answering an inane question. Strange, he thought. They never gave away secondhand cars. The prizes were always *brand new*.

"Crap," he said irritably and switched it off.

He showered and rang Violet. "Have you found out where Markos has his warehouse yet?"

"And a very good morning to you, Harry. And no, I haven't. I'm searching the Land Registry. If it's listed, I should have an answer for you soon. Have you heard from Jason? Has he made contact?"

"I've heard nothing so far. But it's early yet. Give him time to get his skis on."

"I fear time may be running out for Alice," Violet said.

"We're going as fast as we can, Vi. I've even involved the Metropolitan Police to try and speed up the search a bit."

"Drastic measures. Was that necessary?"

"Drastic, yes, but they came to me initially. They're dealing with what they think might be a ritual sacrifice. It could be linked to Anton Markos and the Children of Hecate."

"Oh, dear God!"

"Don't worry, Vi. It wasn't Alice. Just another poor girl."

Violet gave a loud sigh of relief. "What's the likelihood of Markos being involved?"

"I'd say about ninety per cent, possibly more. From what Martin's been able to find out, the Children are the only sect, cult, whatever you want to call them, operating in London. I need that address, Vi."

"I'm surprised your Martin hasn't checked the Land Registry records."

"He might have done, but I haven't been into the office yet. I'm leaving now. I want you to check, just to verify."

"Hey, Harry," Martin said as Harry strolled into his office.

"Had any luck tracing the warehouse?"

Martin shook his head. "I can't find anything on the Land Registry owned by either Erik Strasser or Anton Markos."

"No. Vi was trying as well. She'll draw a blank too, no doubt." Harry rubbed his chin.

"How good is her intel that there actually *is* a warehouse?"

"Well, she was right about the apartment in Clerkenwell and the house in Fairford."

"But we don't know she's right about the warehouse. The problem is, once the development schemes got underway, most of the warehouses were either pulled down to make way for housing, or the buildings were redeveloped and turned into apartments. I've searched as far out as Dagenham and Shoreditch for any property twenty thousand square yards and above. There are a few dotted about throughout the area, but nothing with Strasser/Markos name attached."

"Let me call her." He pulled out his phone and dialed Violet's number. "Vi, how positive are you about the warehouse?"

"Is your boy having problems tracking it down?"

"Yes."

"Good. So am I. I was beginning to doubt my skills."

"So the warehouse is a definite?"

"Is anything definite in this life?"

"Vi! I'm trying to help you here?"

"Sorry. I'm not being flippant. This is just getting to me. All I can think about is my niece, alone with that scumbag."

"Well," Harry said. "Clear your head and tell me. Are you sure this warehouse actually exists?"

"I'm sure. My source is unimpeachable."

"But you're not going to tell me who it is?"

"It doesn't matter who it is, Harry. The intelligence is sound. Bye, Harry." She rang off.

"Bloody woman!" Harry snapped, drawing looks from Maggie and Christine. "Yes, Martin," he said more evenly. "Her intel is good."

"Well, perhaps we're going about this the wrong way. If you were renting or buying a warehouse, or something similar, that you're going to use for nefarious purposes…"

Harry raised his eyebrows. "*Nefarious purposes?*"

"You know what I mean. Well, it stands to reason that you wouldn't use your own name."

Harry thought for a moment. "Yes, I can see that. But that leaves us with even less of a clue than before."

"As I said, perhaps we're going about this the wrong way." He tapped a few keys and waited as the screen on his desk filled with lines of text divided into two holding boxes. "Right," he said. "The box on the right, properties within a five-mile radius of the center of Docklands. The box on the left, the names of the owners or tenants."

Harry let his gaze drift down the list of names. After a few seconds he said, "There," and tapped the screen with his finger. "Omicron Limited."

Martin looked at it questioningly.

"Omicron. The fifteenth letter of the Greek alphabet."

Martin smiled. "I'm impressed."

"Probably the only benefit of a classical education."

"Let me search it on the Companies House website," Martin said and started hitting keys again.

The screen lit up again. "There you go. Omicron. Registered owner one Anton Markos. Importers of olive oil."

"Got him," Harry said. "Address?"

"Unit 14, Hawk Lane Industrial Estate, Barking." He called up Google Maps. "It's on the river, if that's any help."

"Well done, Martin," Harry said with a grin and patted Martin on the shoulder and went back to McKinley's office. "John, fancy a trip?"

"Somewhere exotic?"

"An industrial estate in Barking, Essex."

McKinley shrugged. "You take me to all the best places," he said.

"Susan."

"Hello, Mr. Bai…Harry. What can I do for you?"

"Omicron Limited. It's a sham company, owned by Markos. A warehouse in Barking."

"Address?" she said, and jotted it on the blotter next to the other two addresses as Harry read it out to her. "I don't suppose you can wait for me to apply for a search warrant?"

"You won't get one. No grounds. I'm driving over there now," Harry said. "I'll meet you there if you're interested."

He disconnected and turned to McKinley. "Get your coat, John,"

Chapter Sixteen

Jason met her on the nursery slopes of the Kitzbühelerhorn Mountain. Dressed from head to toe in red, her hair tucked inside a woolen hat, mirror-lensed shades covering her eyes, she stood outside the postcard-perfect chalet where skiers could buy refreshments, holding a white card with his name on it. He skied across to her. "Fraulein Metz?" he said.

She dropped the card in a nearby waste bin and gripped his gloved hand in both of hers. "Karin, please. Good day, Herr West," she said and shook his hand. "Is it your first visit to Austria?"

"Call me Jason. No, just my first time in Kitzbühel. I've been to Austria before, but never visited the Tyrol. It's very beautiful."

He wasn't exaggerating. The sweeps of snow-clad mountains were breathtaking. Dotted with picturesque, Swiss-style chalets and spiky pine trees, set in white, against a bright blue sky, the Austrian Tyrolean region was one of the world's most stunning holiday destinations.

Karin Metz smiled. "And it snowed last night, so the skiing is very good today." Her English was good but heavily accented. He didn't need telling about the snowfall. As he'd walked to the slopes this morning, snow had swallowed his boots and soaked into the legs of his ski pants.

Karin gripped the finger of her glove with her teeth, shook her head and pulled it off. She took a small notebook from her pocket and flipped it open. "I have you down as intermediate. When did you last ski?"

"A few years ago. I need you to tell me what I'm doing wrong."

She nodded her head vigorously. "Yes, I can do that. Come," she said, "to the lift."

They skied together across to the chairlift, a continuous loop of cable with chairs hanging down from it, carrying skiers up the mountain to the various runs.

"Take the lift up to the first slope and ski down from there. I'll stand here and watch you. Okay?" Karin said.

"Fine," he said, and hopped aboard the first pair of seats that came past.

He reached the top of the slope, alighted, moved his way across, settled himself and pushed off with his ski poles. The slope was quite gentle, but with the cold wind ripping past his face and the hiss of his skis over the crisp snow, it was only a matter of seconds before the adrenaline started coursing through his veins, making him feel exhilarated and slightly light-headed. He reached the bottom where Karin was standing, and snowplowed to a stop.

She was watching him closely. "Not bad," she said. "Next, we go up together and I'll show you what is wrong with your...standing?"

"Stance."

"Yes, stance. Come on." She led the way and he followed her across to the chairlift again. They boarded the lift together and sat side by side as it carried them up the mountain. "We go slightly higher this time, yes?"

"That's good for me." He sat back and stared across at the neighboring peaks, noticing the adrenaline rush subside slightly. He could feel the warmth of her body through the layers of clothing. She was extremely pretty. Even with no makeup and her hair hidden from view, she possessed a pure, fresh-faced beauty, and he found his anger at Anton Markos start to flow through him, replacing the adrenaline in his bloodstream.

"Here," she said and stepped off the lift. "Right, let's try that again."

"We'll take my car," McKinley said. "I'll drive."

"Fine," Harry said, opened the passenger door of John McKinley's Audi RS5 and got in.

"Do you have the address?"

Harry had it in his pocket on a scrap of paper. He found it and read it out while McKinley tapped it into his GPS. Soon they were heading east across London.

The Hawk Lane Industrial Estate had little to recommend it. Set in a fairly run-down part of the borough, it consisted of rows of featureless units, interspersed with larger, and just as bland, warehouses.

They found Omicron Ltd in the northwest corner. There was nothing to differentiate it from any of the other warehouses on the estate, apart from a white laminated sign with the name in gold capital letters and a rather crude drawing of an olive tree. But the warehouse was probably the biggest on the estate, built in cinder block with a green metal roof, and about the size of a small aircraft hangar. It looked deserted.

McKinley stopped the car on a large concrete rectangle, and both men stepped out.

"It doesn't look like DI Tyler's here yet," Harry said.

"Are we going to wait for her?"

Harry shrugged and walked across to the large steel double doors at the front of the building. There was a small Judas gate set in the right-hand door that had a multidigit combination lock. He tried the handle but it didn't budge.

"Not a lock I can pick," McKinley said.

Set in the wall, either side of the door and nine feet from the ground, were a row of windows, each window a two-foot square of glass, with no visible means of opening them.

Harry and McKinley stood back, wondering how to get inside. "Have you got anything in the trunk to force the door?" Harry said.

McKinley shook his head. "A jack and a tire iron, not much else."

A dark blue Ford made its way down the service road towards them. As it reached the warehouse, it swung onto the concrete rectangle and drew to a halt next to McKinley's Audi. Susan Tyler and Jake Bartlett stepped out and joined the two men.

"What have we got?" Susan said to Harry.

"There doesn't seem to be anyone here," he said.

She clicked her tongue. "We need to see inside," she said, looking up at the windows. "They're too high. We need something to stand on. Jake, move the car and park it under the windows."

Bartlett threw her a mock salute and got back in the car. Jake Bartlett looked to be in his forties, tall and muscular, with a wide face and a flat nose. It was a face that had seen far too many bar brawls, but the dark brown eyes seemed kind, and they sparkled with good humor.

He started the car and drove it round until it was directly under the right-hand set of windows. He got out of the car, climbed onto the hood and stepped from the hood to the roof. The windows were now level with his chest. He crouched slightly and peered through one of the glass squares, and then moved along to look through another.

"What do you see, Jake?"

"Cushions," he said. "Cushions all over the floor. There's something against the side wall, but I can't make it out. It's too dark in there. Wait. There's something else on the floor."

"What?"

"Don't know."

Susan reached into the car and said, "Try with this," and handed him a long metal flashlight.

Bartlett took the flashlight from her and shone it through the window. "Whatever it is, it's catching the light. It looks wet, a puddle of something. Could be oil. It is meant to be an olive oil warehouse after all."

"Could it be blood?" Harry said.

Bartlett moved back to the first window and shone the beam down to illuminate the floor.

"Yes," he said quietly after a few moments. "I think is."

"Come down, Jake," Susan said. "Let's figure out how to get inside." Her police officer instincts were crying out to get inside as fast as possible. Wetness on a floor under these circumstances was likely to mean just one thing - she was certain it was blood.

Jake Bartlett climbed down and the four of them stood staring at the door, looking for a solution.

"We could always break a window and climb through," McKinley said.

"And how would the person that climbs through get out again if the doors don't open from the inside?"

"You've got me there," McKinley said.

"Who are you again? I recognize your face...and your height."

"Sorry," Harry said. "John McKinley. A colleague. You met last year when we came to the station."

Susan stuck out her hand. "DI Tyler," she said.

"Yeah, I remember."

"DS Bartlett," Bartlett said.

"Well, that's the introductions out of the way. Now, how the hell are we going to get inside?" Harry said.

"I'll check the rear—see if there's a way in there." McKinley ducked around the side of the building and disappeared from view.

"Have you got anything with you that you can use to force the door?" Harry said.

"Nothing of much use. I wasn't expecting to be breaking and entering," Bartlett said.

"Me neither."

"Round here!" McKinley shouted from the back of the warehouse. The three of them started to run, following his voice.

They found McKinley at the back of the building, standing in front of another door: wood, not metal. It looked like any domestic outside door.

"Locked?" Harry said.

"Yes, but look." McKinley grabbed the door handle and shook. The door moved in its frame. "I don't need to be clever about it."

"Break it down," Susan said.

McKinley took a step backwards and kicked out at the door. The lock offered no resistance. With the sound of splintering wood and a squeal of rusted hinges, the door swung inwards. Harry stepped through the opening. "Come on," he said.

They found themselves in a small kitchen area. There was a stainless steel sink, a fridge, but not much else, not even a kettle. They carried on through to an equally small office space, but all it contained was a plywood desk and an empty filing cabinet.

"Hardly the office of a thriving business," Susan said.

"It wasn't here that the work was being done," Harry said. He'd moved through another door and now stood in the main part of the warehouse.

"What's with all the cushions?" McKinley said glancing around at the small pads littering the floor.

"They're hassocks," Harry said. He saw the blank expression on Bartlett's face. "Pew cushions, kneelers. This is a place of worship."

Susan swung her flashlight to illuminate the sidewall.

"There's the wet patch I saw I saw," Bartlett said, pointing to a sticky pool of red, surrounding what looked like a large block of stone. "Definitely blood."

"It's some kind of altar. What were they worshipping?" Susan swung the light up, gasped and took a step back. The stone altar was covered by a red-streaked white sheet. The sheet was covering something else. A shape lying on the altar.

"Shit!" Harry said and walked across to it.

"We should call forensics and get them down here," Susan said.

Harry ignored her. All he could think was how he was going to break the news to Violet. He took hold of the edge of the bloodstained sheet.

"You should wait, Harry," McKinley said.

"Like hell," Harry said, threw back the sheet and stood staring at the mutilated body lying on the stone block.

"What the -?" Susan said and shone the flashlight at the corpse.

Harry was swaying slightly, all his certainty gone as he tried to come to terms with what he was seeing.

"What is it, Harry?" McKinley said.

As Susan swung the flashlight onto the dead face, Harry said, "John, I'd like to introduce you to Anton Markos, otherwise known as Eric Strasser."

Susan aimed the flashlight on the wall. In Markos's blood, someone had drawn a large, red crescent on the cinder blocks.

"Now what?" she said.

Chapter Seventeen

They came down the slope parallel to each other and finished together at the bottom. Karin was laughing. "You've improved a great deal in two hours, Jason."

"The benefit of having an excellent teacher," he said.

"You flatter me," she said.

"Let me buy you dinner tonight, by way of a thank-you."

She shook her head. "You're very kind, but I'm afraid the hotel does not encourage fraternization between instructors and their guests," she said.

"Then we won't tell them."

"I couldn't. I could lose my job."

"I'm only here for three nights. The day after next, I'll be walking the gloomy London streets and wishing I was back breathing alpine air."

"Three nights?"

"Yes."

She looked at her watch. "I must go. I'm late for my next student. Thank you, Jason. It was fun today." She inclined her head and pushed away on her skis.

"Gallo's," he called after her. "I've booked a table for eight o'clock."

She looked back at him and gave a shrug. "I can't."

"Well, I'll be there. I hope you are too," he shouted to her disappearing silhouette.

And if she wasn't? Well, he was here for two more nights. Plenty of time.

He'd just entered his hotel room and flopped down on the king-size bed when his cell phone rang.

"Harry. How are things your end?"

"We found Markos today."

"Really?" he said, feeling his spirits start to sink. "Do you want me to cut this short?"

"No. We found Markos, but he's dead. We still haven't found Alice, so the search goes on. Have you made contact with the girl yet?"

"I've just got back from a very pleasant two hours with her on the slopes."

"Did you find out anything? We still need to learn everything we can about Markos: his motivations, what made him tick. Anything that might give us a lead to where Alice is. When are you seeing her again?"

"Hopefully tonight. I booked a table first thing this morning on the off chance."

"Why do you say *hopefully*?"

"Because dating guests is against company policy."

"Do you think she'll show up?"

"I hope so, or else I'll have to book another lesson, and my legs are aching like a sonofabitch after today."

"Well, good luck."

"How did he die?"

"I won't know until I speak to the pathologist, but it was pretty brutal. His flesh was cut up like hamburger. Enjoy your dinner." He rang off.

"Thanks for that, Harry." Jason lay back on the pillow and closed his eyes. Within seconds he was asleep.

"What killed him, Duncan?" Harry said into the phone.

McBride, the Home Office pathologist, frowned. "Between the two of you, you and Detective Inspector Tyler are making my life very hectic. What's the story there, Harry? I thought the department didn't use outside agencies."

"It's mutually beneficial, though whether it will continue, now Markos is dead, is open to speculation. Well?"

"The body was a mess—a massive loss of blood from wounds that were inflicted ante mortem. He must have suffered horribly. I'm still trying to find out what was used to cause those kinds of injuries, but as yet my findings are inconclusive."

"What's your best guess?"

"Harry, you know me better than that. I don't speculate. I deal in facts. All I can tell you is what actually killed him."

"Go on."

"Cause of death was a single stab wound to the aorta. I say *to* the aorta, but actually what pierced his chest went right through his heart and came out the other side."

"A knife like the one that killed Kerry Green?"

"No, nothing like that. That knife left a star-shaped entry wound, and you could see tearing of the surrounding tissue as it was removed. No, whatever penetrated Mr. Markos's heart was something cylindrical and about three-eighths of an inch in diameter: a rod of some kind, metal, wood, maybe fiberglass. Whatever it was left no residue in the wound. It was a very clean hole. Thinking about it, it could be a glass spear. We're still running tests. I'll let you know as soon as I have something more definite."

"Time of death?"

"Ah, that I can pin down by his liver temperature," McBride said. "Between the hours of two and four this morning."

"Any drugs in his system?"

"The toxicology report has come back negative for drugs, prescription or otherwise. Your boy was clean."

"Okay, Professor. Call me when you've got a better idea about the weapons used."

"We've got the footage you wanted from Traffic," Gillian said as Susan and Bartlett arrived back at the station.

"Is it something we can use?" she said.

"It's in the player in the incident room."

"Get everyone in there. We'll watch it together."

Five minutes later the incident room was packed. Bartlett switched on the television and pressed Play on the DVD player. There was a short run of blank white screen, and then they were sitting and standing, watching footage of Waterloo Bridge taken at three fifteen the previous morning.

There was no traffic on the bridge until a car drove along and stopped on the westbound carriageway. A figure dressed in a black hoodie got out of the car, went around to the rear, opened the trunk and pulled out a lifeless body of a girl. Hoisting the corpse onto his shoulder, the figure took two steps and launched the body into space over the side of the bridge. Then, without looking back, the figure slammed the trunk shut, climbed back behind the wheel and drove away. The whole incident had taken less than two minutes.

"Play it again," Susan said.

Bartlett pressed Play again and the footage repeated.

"And again. And I want you all to watch carefully and tell me if there's something we can use to help us find Kerry Green's killer, because I'm fucked if I can see anything useful."

They watched it again. When it stopped, Susan said, "Well?"

"It's a light blue Peugeot 207. We'll have the plate once this goes down to the lab."

"It's probably stolen," Susan said. "He drives onto the bridge, bold as brass, and parks in clear view of the camera, dumps the body and drives off. He was making no effort to hide what he was doing. He doesn't care, thinks he's fireproof."

"You can't get a look at his face," Witherspoon said. "It's hidden by his hood."

"You can't even tell if it's male or female. Could be a girl," Tom Fox said.

"A bloody strong one if it is. Hauls that body out of the trunk as if it's a rag doll," Bartlett said.

"So basically nothing we can use," Susan said. There was silence in the room. "No, I thought not. It's been that kind of day. Jake, get down to that club in Soho and show Kerry's photo around. Take Brian with you. I think it's about bloody time our luck changed. If anyone wants me, I'll be in my office." She stalked out of the room, slamming the door behind her.

She walked into her office and closed the door, sat down at her desk, took out her electronic cigarette and started puffing on it furiously. What a godawful day, she thought and stared down at her hands. They were visibly shaking. Every time she closed her eyes, all she could see was the butchered body of Anton Markos lying on the stone altar. She stood again and rushed to the toilet, barely making it through the door before she threw up.

"Come in and close the door, Harry," Crozier said.

Harry walked into Crozier's office and shut the door behind him. He sat down at the desk, feeling every inch the errant schoolboy hauled up in front of the headmaster.

"Are you losing control of this?"

"I'm not sure what you mean."

"Don't be bloody coy with me. You know exactly what I mean. You have a member of the public living the high life in Austria at our expense; you're letting Violet Bulmer lead you by the nose—"

"That's not fair, Simon. Vi has—"

"Shut up, Harry. I haven't finished. You're letting Violet Bulmer lead you by the nose through this case. And you've involved the Met in one of our investigations. I've just had Deputy Commissioner Mackie on the phone, tearing me a new one because you're involving his force without going through the correct channels."

"Can't you get the Home Secretary to have a word in his ear? Quiet him down?"

"I can do that and will probably *have* to do that. But you're missing the point. You're leaving us very exposed here. The press is already sniffing around at Barking, threatening to break the story in the nationals. The wrong people are starting to ask the wrong sort of questions. So I ask again, are you in control of this?"

"Inasmuch as I can be," Harry said.

"What kind of answer is that? I expect this kind of escalating mess from Robert Carter. I don't expect it from you."

Harry crossed and uncrossed his legs. He took a deep breath and measured his words carefully.

"West is a very good investigator. I've been watching him develop over the last few years. In fact he's *so* good, I'm going to recommend he join us full-time when he gets back from Austria. Vi's a valuable outside asset. She isn't *leading me by the nose*, as you put it. She's brought some things to our attention, that's all. I'm following through."

"Yes, with her leading you by the nose."

Harry glared at him. "And Detective Inspector Tyler came to me for help, not the other way round, so if Mackie wants to go around chewing people's ears off, he should start looking in his own backyard first."

Crozier looked at Harry steadily. "Finished?"

Harry opened his mouth to speak again, but snapped it shut.

"Good. Harry, I'm not being unreasonable here. I know events can unfold in ways you don't expect. I'm just asking that you be more circumspect in the future. Department 18 works because it operates under the radar. By involving outside people and outside agencies, we leave ourselves open to scrutiny, by the media and by people higher up the governmental food chain than me. Understand?"

Harry nodded.

"So where are you taking the hunt for Alice Logan next?"

"You want me to carry on then?"

"Of course I want you to carry on. We offered Vi Bulmer our help. It would be churlish to withdraw that offer. We agree that she's been a great asset to us in the past, and I want that to continue, so we'll do what we can to help her. Just tighten the reins and don't let her run the operation. This is a Department 18 investigation. Don't let other people hijack it. And if the press come sniffing around…"

Harry gave him an *are you kidding me?* look.

"Well, I've made you aware of my feelings."

"Thanks for sharing. Anything else?"

"Just go and do your job, Harry."

"That's what I've been trying to do," Harry said bleakly. He got up and walked out of Crozier's office. The most galling thing was, Crozier was right.

The telephone rang on Susan's desk. What now? She picked it up. "DI Tyler."

"It's Harry. Do you fancy going out for a drink tonight? There are a few things I'd like to run by you."

"Haven't you had enough for one day?"

"Yes, actually I have, but I'd still like to take you for a drink. Do you know the Wellington in Bridge Street?"

"I know it. It's five minutes away."

"Meet you there in about half an hour?"

"Okay," she said and put down the phone, picked up her electronic cigarette and inhaled deeply.

Chapter Eighteen

Not for the first time in his life, Crozier felt conflicted. He felt he had no choice but to allow Harry to continue his investigation. He trusted Harry's instincts, but he also knew that Harry's main weakness was that he often thought with his gut and not his head. Sometimes Crozier had to ignore their friendship and pull rank. Increasingly he was finding it a difficult thing to do.

"Trudy," he said into the intercom on his desk. "Hold my calls. I'll be out of the office for an hour."

"You're late for your appointment with Dr. Merriman."

"Exactly. That's where I'll be if you need me."

He walked out of his office and took the elevator up to the next floor. Here the layout was softer, less formal than in the rest of the building. He walked along the corridor to an office that looked more like somebody's lounge than a place of work. The door was open and he could see Dr. Julia Merriman sitting, relaxed in her office chair, legs crossed, leather-bound textbook open and propped up on her knee.

He tapped on the door.

She looked up from the book and beckoned him inside. "Come in, Simon," she said.

Crozier entered the wood-paneled office. She put the book down on a coffee table, picked up a yellow legal pad and rose from her seat to greet him.

Julia Merriman was in her early forties, tall and effortlessly elegant. Her honey-colored hair was swept back from her face in a timeless chignon. "Take a seat," she said and indicated a black leather chair opposite her own.

She waited until Crozier sat down, adjusted the knife-edge crease on the trousers of his Savile Row suit and made himself comfortable, and then she sat herself and opened the legal pad and consulted her notes.

"Sorry I'm late. I had a meeting," Crozier said.

"No problem. Coffee?"

He shook his head "No thanks. So, Julia, am I making progress quickly enough for you?"

"It's been sixteen months since you were attacked, Simon. It was a life-changing, traumatic event. Do you think you've made progress quickly enough?"

"I'm not really sure what benefits these therapy sessions are meant to be."

Julia adjusted her spectacles on the bridge of her nose and stared at him over the top of them. There was a slight smile playing on her lips. "I've heard that you're a new man," she said. "More relaxed, less irritable, more patient. Do you think that's a fair assessment?"

"Well. That would depend who you've been speaking to."

Her smile widened. "I never reveal my sources," she said. "But I find it useful to discover how you're being perceived by the people you work with. It gives me a clearer impression of the progress you're making."

"So are you ready to sign off on these sessions and let me get back to work?"

"These sessions are mandatory in cases where an operative's life has been on the line," Julia said.

"I know," Crozier said. "It was me who instigated them five years ago."

"Then you should appreciate the benefits of them."

"I introduced them for my operatives, who often find themselves risking their lives during the course of their work. Not for me, who, for most of the time, sits behind a desk and directs the operations."

"Then I would have thought these sessions would be even more important for someone in your position. Why are you so eager to bring them to a close? Don't you enjoy them?"

"I don't think *enjoy* is the appropriate term. I've found them enlightening, and they've helped me reassess my life since the attack, to help me realize what is important and what is trivial."

"Then not such a waste of time?"

Crozier smiled and shook his head. "No, I suppose not. And you're cheaper than Harley Street."

Julia scribbled something down on her pad. "Right then, shall we begin?"

"Very well," Crozier said, settled back in his chair and crossed his legs.

The music was loud enough to make the floorboards throb in the Abyss.

Bartlett and Witherspoon moved through the gyrating bodies on the dance floor, flashing Kerry Green's picture to little or no response. They rendezvoused at the bar. Bartlett ordered a whiskey, Witherspoon lemonade.

"Ever felt out of place?" Witherspoon said.

"Like a nun in a monastery," Bartlett agreed.

Witherspoon sipped his lemonade. "Do you see who's down the bar from us? Three o'clock."

Bartlett turned his head and looked along the length of the bar "Terry Butler," he said quietly. "Did you know he was into this scene?"

"I thought mugging old ladies was more his form of entertainment."

There was a girl hanging on to Butler's arm. Too young to be drinking, bleached blonde hair and smudged eye makeup. "Who's that with him?"

"Never seen her before," Bartlett said. "Come on, let's go and have a chat with them."

They moved along the bar and pulled in next to Butler and the girl.

"Hello, Terry. You into this death rock scene?"

Butler picked up his glass and tried his best to ignore them. Witherspoon grabbed his arm and forced it back to the bar before Butler could take a sip. "Don't be rude, Terry. I said hello."

"'Lo," Butler said.

Bartlett pulled the photograph from his pocket and held it out for them both to see. Butler looked at it blankly, but the girl pulled the photograph from

Bartlett's fingers and looked at it closely. "That's Kezza."

"Kezza?"

"Kezza. Kerry Green. She was in here the other night. Left with a friend of yours, Terry. Fin whatever-his-name-is. Is she all right? I haven't seen her since then. Has she been in an accident?"

"She's dead," Witherspoon said.

The girl's face blanched.

"Dead? How?"

"Murdered."

"Shit."

"We'd like both of you to come back to Waterloo Road station with us, to give a statement."

Butler was poised, ready to run. Witherspoon tightened his grip on his arm. "Don't even think about it, Terry."

Butler looked to the girl and mouthed, "Stupid bitch."

Witherspoon saw that the girl was confused, as much by Terry's anger at her as by the presence of the two policemen and their request. She'd probably never been in trouble with the police before.

"I'll miss my train," she said weakly.

"We'll get someone to take you home afterwards," Bartlett said. "Come on. Our car's outside."

The Wellington public house in Bridge Street was a relic of a bygone age. Resisting all efforts to modernize and turn it into a gastro-pub, or worse, the landlord had retained most of his regular patrons and added to their number by attracting those looking for an adult evening, free of bland, piped music and families with unruly preteens whose idea of going to the pub was to run from table to table and annoy as many people as possible.

Harry ordered tonic water from the bar and found a corner booth from where he could watch the door. Susan walked in before he had drunk halfway down the glass.

He stepped out of the booth, caught her eye and beckoned her over to the bar. "Glad you could make it," he said. "What can I get you?"

"White wine spritzer, please."

Harry attracted the barman's attention and ordered her drink.

"Not drinking, Harry?"

He pointed to the glass of tonic water sitting on the table in the booth. "I'm good."

The barman set the glass down in front of Susan. She picked it up, took a sip and followed Harry back to the booth.

"I've walked past this place lots of times but never come inside. I thought it was an old man's pub."

"It is," Harry said. "I'm an old man."

"I wouldn't have said so. What are you? Mid fifties?"

"Round about."

"That's not old."

"Kind, but I think I've aged ten years after today."

"It *was* pretty gruesome," she said, and started to take her electronic cigarette out of her bag.

He moved and covered her hand with his own. "Sorry," he said. "They don't allow them in here."

She sighed and let the cigarette drop back in the bag.

"That's what makes these bloody things so pointless. You can't use them on planes, in pubs and restaurants. What are we quitters supposed to do?"

"Go outside with the regular smokers and freeze your tits off while you suck."

"Is that progress?"

"No, but it's much better for you."

"If you say so." She smiled. "Were you as shocked as you seemed, finding Markos like that?"

"It wasn't what I expected to find. I thought it was going to be Alice Logan under that sheet."

"I must admit, that was what I feared," Susan said.

"She's still missing."

"Yes, I realize that. Do you still want my help trying to find her, or have you brought it all in under Department 18 business?"

Harry didn't answer. He took a swig of his tonic water and shuddered slightly.

"Are you okay?" she said.

"This stuff is not the same when it's not diluted with vodka."

Someone chose a song on the jukebox menu and Elvis started to croon.

"God," Susan said. "This takes me back. I never got into the Vegas Elvis, but he was a hunk before he started wearing white jumpsuits."

"I'm surprised you're old enough to remember."

"You're not Irish, are you?"

Harry shook his head.

"Only you're full of the old blarney."

"I lived out there for a while. Maybe it rubbed off on me."

She laughed.

Off duty, Susan was much easier to be with. He had thought twice before asking her to come for a drink, but he had a feeling that beneath the no-nonsense, prickly persona, there was a much softer side to her.

"How long did you live in Ireland?"

"A few years, after I quit the department."

"You quit?"

"Oh yes, I quit."

"May I ask why?"

He shook his head. "Do you like being in the police?"

"It's a job and I'm good at it. I'm not much good at anything else. My house looks like a bomb's hit it, and I'm a lousy cook. I live on TV dinners and takeouts most of the time."

"Yes, well, I'm guilty of that too. You'll have to let me buy you dinner sometime."

"Are you asking me out on a date, Harry?"

"I thought I already had."

"And I thought you had some things to discuss about the cases we're working on."

"That too," Harry said with a smile.

"Where do you think Alice could be?"

The smile was wiped from his face and his eyes clouded. "I really haven't got a clue."

"You should start with Markos's apartment in Clerkenwell and his house in the Cotswolds. You might find pointers there to where she's gone."

"Yes," he said. "You're right. Do you think Markos was responsible for Kerry Green's murder?"

"That was what I was thinking, which is why I trekked over to Barking."

"And now?"

"Now, I'm not so sure. There's definitely a connection. Someone painted a crescent in blood on the wall of the warehouse, and a crescent was carved on Kerry's body. It could be a coincidence, but it's a bit of a stretch. At the same time, traffic cameras on Waterloo Bridge filmed someone dropping Kerry's body into the Thames at three fifteen the night before last. I couldn't see the face, but it was a much smaller figure than Anton Markos. From the photo in the file you gave me and from what I saw today, I would put him at a bit more than six feet. The person on the bridge I would estimate a good six inches shorter."

"How did you arrive at that?"

"The person was driving a Peugeot 207. I judged his height by comparing him to the height of the car when he was dragging Kerry's body from the trunk."

Harry nodded slowly. "Fair enough. But if not Markos, who?"

"And that, Harry, is the 64,000-dollar question. I've got my guys out tonight showing her picture around at the Abyss. It's a Goth nightclub. She had the club's reentry stamp on the back of her hand, so we know she was there. If anyone saw her there, we might find out who was the last person to see her."

"Clever," Harry said.

"It's called police work. Can I get you another drink?"

"Same again, please."

"Tonic water? Don't you drink?"

"Not anymore."

Susan gave him a look that said, *I know what you mean, but I'm not going there.* He appreciated that. He found himself beginning to like Susan Tyler—like her very much.

"Tracy...may I call you Tracy?"

The girl from the nightclub nodded. She looked very young sitting in the interview room—young and frightened.

"Tracy, let me say that you're not in any trouble," Witherspoon said. "You are here voluntarily as a witness. You're free to walk out that door at any time, but we would appreciate any help you can give us with our inquiries."

"Okay," she said in a very small voice.

"You say you saw Kerry Green, Kezza, at the club the night before last."

"That's right."

"And she was with someone called Fin. Did they seem okay to you? Were they arguing? Did she seem distressed in any way?"

"She didn't. Nah, she seemed happy, really made up to be with him."

"And this Fin, you don't remember his name?"

"Nah. I've seen him at the club before and I know Terry knows him." Her gaze drifted to the ceiling as if she was looking there for the answer to Witherspoon's question. "It was something Irish. Clancy, something like that."

A light went on in Witherspoon's brain. "Clusky? Was it Clusky? Fin Clusky?"

"Could be...yeah...that sounds right."

"Good girl," Witherspoon said.

Tracy smiled wanly.

Chapter Nineteen

"Fin Clusky," Witherspoon said out in the hall. "Finbar bloody Clusky."

"You sound as if you know him," Bartlett said.

"Oh, I know him," Witherspoon said. "Nasty little shit. He glues the wings on flies, just to have the pleasure of ripping them off again. Claims his dad was a soldier in the IRA, but according to his mother, his real father was a merchant seaman from Bradford, and Fin was the product of a one-night stand. What's Terry saying?"

"Not a lot. Says he didn't see Kerry with anyone at the club that night. Swears blind he doesn't know anybody called Fin."

"He's lying," Witherspoon said.

"Of course he is, but proving it isn't vital to the investigation at the moment. If the girl says Kerry Green left the club with Clusky that night, then that's enough to be going on with," Jake Bartlett said.

"Shall we send them home?"

"Might as well. Organize a car to take them."

Jason West sat at a table in Gallo's bistro for most of the evening, admiring the minimalist decor, with its zebra stripes and mosaics, and enjoying a well-cooked steak. But he ate alone. Karin didn't show. At eleven he went back to the hotel. He'd call Harry in the morning and give him the bad news.

At the desk, he asked for his key. It was a different receptionist from yesterday, a younger woman wearing modern attire. She handed him a key and said, "Your ski lesson is booked for eleven, Herr West. The same as today."

"But I didn't book a lesson," he said. " I was going to wait to see how it went."

The receptionist pulled out the appointment book and ran her finger down the page. She looked up at him with a smile. "Here it is. Eleven a.m. Herr West. Two hours instruction with Karin."

He shook his head. "Thank you. It must have slipped my mind."

The woman looked at him oddly, then shrugged and placed the appointment book back under the desk. "Sleep well, Herr West."

"Thank you," Jason said and took the elevator back to his room, his spirits lifting as he ascended.

"Where have you parked your car?" Harry said as they left the pub.

"Back at the station. You?"

"I walked."

"Far?"

"Just over a mile."

"Do you want a ride home?"

Harry looked up at the sky. A thin drift of rain dampened his face. "Would you mind?"

"I wouldn't have offered if I did," she said. "Come on, the station's just around the corner."

They reached the car park just in time to see Jake Bartlett emerge from the station and walk towards his car. He stopped when he saw them.

"Hi, Jake," Susan said. "How did it go at the club?"

Jake walked across to them. "Got a witness who saw Kerry Green leave the pub with a lowlife called Finbar Clusky at about ten that evening."

"Clusky, *that* worm?"

"You know him then?" Harry said.

"Oh, I know him. He'd sell his grandmother's dentures if he thought he could make enough money from them to buy drugs. He lives in a council flat over on the Peabody Estate."

"Should I take Brian and go and question him?" Bartlett said.

"Leave it till the morning, Jake. The day's been long enough already."

Bartlett looked at Harry and then at Susan, his mind whirring and making the connection. "You two been somewhere nice?"

"The Wellington," Harry said.

"I'm just going to drive Mr. Bailey home."

"The Wellington. I know it. My old man used to go there to play dominos with his mates."

Susan suppressed a smile. "Good night, Jake."

"Good night, guv. See you in the morning."

"Bright and early."

"*Guv?*" Harry said as Bartlett climbed into his Mondeo and drove from the car park.

"If they called me ma'am, they'd have to tug their forelocks and bow as well. I couldn't handle that." Susan stopped beside a dark green Skoda and clicked the lock button her key fob. "Come on, get in. Let's get you home."

"Would you like to come in for coffee?" Harry said as they reached his apartment block.

"What do the Yanks say? *I'll take a rain check*, if that's okay."

"Fine," Harry said, hiding his disappointment behind an easy smile. "Another time."

He opened the door and made to move out, but she stopped him with a hand on his arm. "I mean it, Harry. Another time, and soon. I've had a really nice evening."

"Sorry we didn't get to play dominos."

She smiled. "We've got the rest of our lives to play dominos," she said and leaned towards him.

He kissed her on the cheek. "Good night, Sue,"

"Good night, Harry, and thanks. I don't do the social thing nearly as much as I should."

He got out of the car and turned up the collar of his coat against the steadily increasing rain. She pulled out onto the road, and he watched until her taillights were just a red blur in the rain, and then he went inside.

"Claws."

"What?"

"You wanted to know what made the wounds on Markos's body."

"Christ, Duncan," Harry said. "What time is it?" He squinted at the green LCD figures on his radio alarm clock.

"A little after eight," McBride said before Harry could bring them into focus. "Don't you sleep?"

"Not when I've got something as interesting as this to work on."

"Claws you say?"

"Yes. It was some kind of animal. A dog, I thought at first, but now I doubt it. It would have to be something like a Rottweiler, but bigger, judging by the spacing between each claw. And there's something else."

"I'm listening."

"Hair. Well, I say hair, but it's more like fur. Some of it's embedded in the wounds. I've taken a sample and couriered it over to London Zoo. Their people may be able to tell us what it is."

"And you have no idea."

"From the ferocity of the attack, I would say some kind of large, wild animal. That's all I can give you. Sorry I can't be more help, unless you know of any wild beasts roaming the streets of Barking."

"Can't help you," Harry said.

"That's what I thought. We'll just have to wait and see what the boffins at Regents Park come up with."

He'd no sooner hung up the phone when it rang again. He picked it up.

"Haven't you got something to tell me, Harry?" It was Violet Bulmer.

"Anton Markos is dead," he said.

"Yes, I know. Jason told me. *He* bothered to call me from Austria and tell me. When were you going to get round to phoning me?"

"It was a busy day, Vi," Harry said, but the truth was he'd been delaying calling her, afraid of upsetting her.

"I'm a big girl. I can take it."

Was she reading his mind again? It wouldn't surprise him. Violet had psychic powers that put his own minor ones into the shade.

"How did he die?"

"A single stab wound through the heart. But his body was mutilated. I've just had the Home Office pathologist on the phone. He suspects Markos was the victim of some kind of attack by a wild animal."

There was silence on the other end of the line. "Vi? Are you still there? Vi?"

"I'm here. Just thinking. Will you be carrying on the search for Alice, now Markos is dead?"

"Of course," he reassured her. "We still need to know what's happened to her. When did you speak to Jason?"

"Late last night."

"How did it go with the girl?"

"She didn't show."

"Shame."

"But she *did* book him another lesson for later this morning."

"Then we shall wait and see if she can throw any light on the world of Anton Markos."

"And what are you going to do next?"

"Go to his apartment in Clerkenwell and have a look round."

"How will you get in?"

"I'll take John McKinley with me. He can pick most locks."

"Then let me know if you find anything interesting. Hell, Harry, let me know if you don't. Just keep me in the picture, okay? Anything is better than the scenarios my imagination conjures up when I'm kept in the dark."

"I will, Vi. I promise."

He got to Whitehall to find McKinley sitting in his office. McKinley had started a fresh thriller. Lee Child.

He put the book down as Harry entered the room.

"Do you fancy some house breaking, John?"

McKinley's face broke into a wide smile. "Damn, Harry. I'll say this: working with you is nothing if not entertaining."

Karin Metz was waiting for Jason outside the refreshment chalet when he arrived on the slopes. She was dressed in the customary red today, but wore no hat. Her silver-blonde hair cascaded over her shoulders. She looked stunning.

"Jason," she said with a smile. "I phoned the hotel to make this appointment. I hope you don't mind."

"Not at all," he said.

The smile faltered. "About last night. I couldn't...the hotel wouldn't understand...and I don't want to lose..."

He held up his hand to stop her. "It's okay, really. I get it. You don't want to lose your job. I understand that. Shall we get on?"

She nodded. "A little higher today perhaps."

"Fine with me."

Within minutes they were sitting in the ski lift, being carried up the mountain.

They reached the highest point they had skied from the day before and Jason made to alight, but she held him back in his seat. "A little higher. We agreed."

Jason relaxed back and let the lift haul them up to the next stage. When they reached it, she said, "One more." And they carried on.

Halfway to the next stage, she turned to him. "Are you working for my grandfather?"

"Pardon? What do you mean?"

"My grandfather, Wolfgang Metz? He's the one keeping me in this ice palace, away from my family and friends. Away from Erik."

Jason's heart sank. Busted. She'd known she was being played, right from the start. Smart girl. He decided to bluff.

"Why do you think that?"

"Because it's obvious you can ski. Certainly to the level I took you to yesterday. And you asked so many questions, about me, about my life. You were checking up on me. Here," she said. "We get off here."

She slipped from the seat and Jason followed. Standing on the compacted snow, with a freezing north wind cutting across the mountain, he looked about him. There was no one up here. They were alone. He saw the sign and his heart began to sink. "This is a black run," he said.

"The only way down the mountain. Perhaps we'll see how good you really are."

"I'm not sure how…"

Her face was suddenly angry, and the true purpose of taking him up so high was revealed. "You're working for my grandfather."

Chapter Twenty

"I don't know what you're talking about," Jason said.

"Liar!" She made a swinging attempt to hit him, but he deflected it with his arm.

"Karin, let's talk about this."

"How much is he paying you to spy on me?"

"You've got the wrong idea," Jason said. "I've never met your grandfather."

She tried to hit him again. Again he blocked it. "Tell me about Erik," he said.

She was breathing heavily, but the venom in her expression eased a little. "I love him," she said. "And he loves me. But Grandfather won't let us be together. He sent Erik away."

"Tell me about him," Jason said, sensing she was calming a little.

"He's a marvelous man, so kind and gentle. And he worships me. He calls me his goddess. His wonderful Hecate."

"Hecate?"

"His pet name for me." She smiled at the memory. "His wonderful, beautiful Hecate. She was a goddess too. He told me."

"Your family is very rich," Jason said. "Perhaps your grandfather was concerned that Erik was only with you for your money."

"No!" she shouted. "He doesn't need my money. Erik is very rich—perhaps even richer than grandfather. It's why I trust him. He loves me for who I am. He doesn't look at me with dollar signs in his eyes."

Jason decided to take a chance. "You're wrong, Karin. You were nothing special to him. There were girls before you—girls who looked at lot like you. And there's another girl, in England. That's where he lives now. There's another girl, another Karin, and he's with her now."

Karin's face turned to stone. "Liar!" she spat, jumped around on her skis and pushed off, tearing down the black run. Within seconds she was a red dot in the distance.

"Shit," Jason said. He'd blown it.

He stood there, with the freezing wind biting at his face, weighing up his options. He could follow Karin down the black run and risk breaking his neck, or he could stay here on the Kitzbühelerhorn and freeze to death.

He heard something creaking above the noise of the wind, and saw the ski lift pass by. He skied across to it and waited for the next pair of chairs. What had brought him up here would carry him down. He might earn a few mocking laughs from the experienced skiers, but that was better than the alternatives. He waited until the chairs were upon him and he mounted, to be carried up, around, and down the mountain.

"I blew it, Harry." He called Harry as soon as he got back to his hotel room.

"What happened?"

Jason told him, almost word for word.

"What did he call her?"

"His wonderful Hecate. That's the name of Markos's followers—the Children of Hecate. So what do you think it means?"

"Obviously, it has great significance to him, but as yet I don't know what."

"What do you want me to do?"

"Come home," Harry said. "Unless you want spend another day skiing."

"No," Jason said. "I've had enough of snow for one winter. I'll call the airline. See if I can use my ticket on another flight."

"Okay. Do you want to tell Vi?"

"I'll call her."

"Right then. I'll see you on your return."

Jason sat on the bed and thought about Karin's pure, porcelain beauty. "Ah," he said to himself after a few moments. "Win some, lose some." And then he tapped in Violet Bulmer's number.

They pulled into a meter space on Goswell Road. McKinley was using the Audi again. It was the most comfortable ride he had ever experienced. The car easily accommodated his long legs.

"Parking in London is a major rip-off," Harry said.

"Tell me about it," McKinley said as he fed coins into the hungry meter. "Can I claim this back on expenses?"

"Fill in the form and give it to Crozier."

"That's a no then."

"Stop bellyaching. The block is up here, on the right."

The apartment building hadn't been standing that long and it looked an expensive place to live—a brushed stainless steel and glass outer shell over a very desirable interior with rich granite flooring and Italian marble walls. It even had its own concierge, an elderly man in a very smart racing-green uniform who sat at a large walnut desk and eyed them suspiciously as they entered the foyer.

"Can I help you, gentlemen?"

Harry produced his Department 18 ID card and waved it under the old man's nose. "We're here to see the person who lives in the penthouse apartment," Harry said.

The old man stared at the official-looking ID card as if mesmerized. "Yes," he said. "Shall I call through to tell him you're here?"

"No. We'll surprise him," McKinley said. They turned and walked towards the elevator.

"You'll need this then. You won't get up there without it." He was holding out what looked like a hotel key card. McKinley walked over to the desk and took it from him. "There's a slot in the control panel," he said. "You'll have to put the card in when you reach the twelfth floor if you want to go up to the penthouse."

"Do I need to enter a PIN number?" McKinley asked.

"Don't worry. The card has a magnetic strip. The panel reads it and identifies it automatically. State of the art," the old man added proudly.

"I'm impressed," McKinley said, and walked back to where Harry was standing at the open elevator doors.

"Is there likely to be any trouble?" the old man called. "Only I have other residents to consider."

"No trouble," Harry called back.

The old man frowned. This place was going downhill. Ever since that flash git moved into the penthouse. Riffraff and undesirables at all hours of the day and night. What was it now? He couldn't comprehend the card Harry had flashed at him. What was Department 18? Some kind of MI5 spin-off? Possibly something to do with Special Branch? He'd had run-ins with the law in his much younger days. Now, when he saw any official-looking laminate, he didn't question it. He really didn't want to know.

McKinley performed the trick with the key card and the elevator carried on upward to the top floor of the building. The doors opened smoothly onto a short corridor with an expensive-looking carpet. The door at the end of the corridor looked robust and gleamed, black with gold door furniture.

McKinley reached into his coat and produced a huge bunch of keys.

"You sure you've got enough there?" Harry said, handing him a pair of latex gloves.

"A key for every occasion," McKinley said "Well, most anyway." He pulled on the gloves, stretching them down over his long, bony fingers. "Bear with me. This might take a while."

It took two minutes.

"Always prepared," McKinley said as he pushed open the door.

"I'd take my hat off to you, John…if I wore one. Come on, let's look around."

The main room of the apartment was large and square, with a deep-pile, cream-colored carpet and a dark purple leather suite. The couch alone would probably cost Harry a month's salary. There was a fifty-inch flat-screen TV and a Bang and Olufsen stereo system with narrow, discreet speakers. A single bookcase stood against the far wall, but held few books, an atlas and a coffee-table book on ceramics being the largest, the rest being rag-bag of self-help guides and an encyclopedia of Greek mythology. A menu for a local Indian restaurant had been used as a bookmark. Harry opened the book at the marked page.

"Hecate," Harry said. "Again. That name is following us around in relation to the Markos case. It's significant, but why?"

"This might answer your question, Harry." McKinley had drifted into the bedroom while Harry was perusing the books.

Harry followed the sound of McKinley's voice and found himself in a room that was essentially a shrine to the Greek goddess. The closed drapes were dark red, as was the cover on the bed, but every available inch of wall space was covered with dramatic posters in gaudy color by painters of variable artistic ability and merit. Interspersed with the posters were monochrome photos of statuary depicting the goddess. A number of the pictures depicted a trio of women, and Harry went to retrieve the encyclopedia. He returned to the bedroom and turned to the relevant page.

"'Hecate is often depicted in triple form, to express her manifold and mystic nature,'" he read.

"But if Markos was obsessed by this particular goddess, why his fixation with blue-eyed blondes? The women in the pictures on the wall all have dark hair."

"I'm ahead of you, John. Look." Harry had put down the book on the bed and pulled open the drapes, and covering the entire window was a single image. It measured twelve feet square and was an image of a woman naked, apart from a diaphanous gown that covered little of her lithe, taut body. The woman in the picture was holding two flaming torches. At the bottom of the picture, in bold capital letters, someone, probably Markos, had written, *"MY HECATE"*.

The woman in the picture had flowing blonde hair and blue eyes, and with daylight from the window diffusing into the room through the picture, the eyes appeared to be glowing. "He obviously had the obsession with Hecate, and a predilection for girls with blonde hair. This picture allowed him to combine and indulge his twin passions. I wonder how old it is?"

"Old enough," McKinley said. "There's printer's mark in the corner and it's in Greek. So he probably had the picture when he lived there and had it shipped around the world with him."

"Unfortunately he's not around to corroborate that, but I think you're probably right. I wonder what a picture like that can do to a young adolescent mind. The image has an undeniable sexual power. That, combined with the hormonal surge puberty brings, probably set him on his path."

"It was my father's copies of *Playboy* that influenced my formative mind," McKinley said.

"*Penthouse* and *Men Only* fueled my masturbatory urges, but we had the advantage, John."

"What was that?"

"We weren't mad."

"And you think Markos was?"

"Psychopathic from a very early age, I'd say, to lead the life he did. The need to control the women he desired probably didn't develop until after puberty, by which time his mania was fully formed. I'd love to know what a real psychologist would make of him."

"Seen enough?"

"Of this, yes, but we've still got to search the place from top to bottom for any clue as to Alice Logan's whereabouts."

McKinley nodded. "Best get started then. You do in here. I'll take the rest of the apartment."

They stepped into the elevator together. "That hasn't moved us forward at all," Bailey said. "Nothing to point us in a direction to even start looking for her."

"And the only thing to suggest she was ever there was a single blonde hair found on the pillow in the bedroom."

"And we're not one hundred per cent sure it's hers. That's why I left it. When the police search the apartment, as they are sure to do, they'll find it. Let them worry about the DNA testing."

"You're not going to give your tame DI the heads up then?"

"Susan Tyler is not my tame anything. And no, I won't say we visited the apartment. That's why I made sure we wore gloves. I don't want our prints going on record as being found there. What we did was illegal. I know it wouldn't be the first time, and I'm as sure as hell it won't be the last. But we can do without muddying the waters right now. Let them get on and do their job."

They passed the desk. The old concierge sat up straight. "All in order?" he said.

"Fine," Harry said. "And if anyone asks, we were never here." He tapped the side of his nose and winked.

"Poor old devil," McKinley said when they got outside. "I'm surprised he didn't salute you."

"I've probably made his day. It'll give him something to talk about with his wife over their cocoa."

Chapter Twenty-One

Clusky sheltered under a tree as he stood and waited for his dealer in the middle of Epping Forest. Not that the tree was making much difference. The rain was still pouring through the bare branches, drumming a tattoo on his crash helmet and running in rivulets down the Plexiglas visor. *Where the fuck is he?* he thought and checked his watch for the third time in the last three minutes.

He was in a clearing, the usual meeting place. He liked this spot because it was hidden from the pathways that walkers used, but was still accessible from the road by bike. The problem was that, because of the dense undergrowth and closely packed trees, it limited his ability to see if his contact was approaching. He pulled out his cell phone to call him, but there was no signal. He swore under his breath and rammed it back in his pocket. He'd give him another five minutes and then he'd go.

A twig snapped behind him and the undergrowth of ferns and bracken rustled. "About bloody time," he said and turned, but there was no one there. Another twig snapped and more rustling. He spun around. "I'm here, you dickhead," he said.

For a moment there was silence, broken only by birdsong, and then the undergrowth began to move, rippling as though something was moving through it. "Stop pissing around," he yelled angrily. "I'm getting soaked here."

And then he heard a low growl coming from somewhere ahead of him. There was an eerie whistle in the air and something smacked into the tree behind him and the bark exploded in a shower of splinters and moss.

He ducked. "Shit!"

Someone was shooting at him. But he hadn't heard a gunshot. The growl sounded again, closer this time. He looked into the trees to see if he could see anyone targeting him, and a pair of red eyes glared back at him out of the shadows.

The eyes were unlike anything he had seen before. "Who's there?" he yelled, an edge of panic to his voice. He looked to his Suzuki, a few yards away, resting on its stand, saddle and fuel tank beaded with rain. He made to run towards it but another whistle and explosion splintered the bark on the tree ahead of him, spinning him round, making him plunge deeper into the trees, away from the clearing, away from his bike, away from escape.

As he ran, the undergrowth around him erupted into life. He glanced to the side and saw the bracken moving as something pursued him. He caught a glimpse of something dark, possibly fur.

He swerved to the left to get away from it. More splinters of tree bark bursting out, close to his face, slicing and stinging, made him cry out and veer back onto his original track. His mind raced, desperately trying to get his bearings.

He had to find the road. In the forest he was an easy target for the things that were hunting him. He swerved again and screamed as something pierced his shoulder, causing a searing, white-hot pain that paralyzed his arm.

He looked down at it. There was a half-inch hole in his leather jacket and blood was pouring from it. He'd been hit.

"Leave me alone, you bastards!" he yelled, and then stopped dead as he saw what was standing in the undergrowth a few feet away from him.

Something huge, covered in thick, dark brown fur—a massive head with a yawning mouth filled with savage yellow teeth, and with glowing red eyes that glared at him ferociously.

He opened his mouth to scream again, not believing what his was seeing, but a matted-furred arm that ended in long, razor-sharp claws lashed out and disemboweled him with one stroke.

Clusky's eyes widened as he stared down at the coils of white intestines spilling out of his ruined belly, and then his eyelids fluttered and closed.

He was dead before he hit the ground.

Susan walked into the incident room, holding a polystyrene cup of coffee. Gillian was by the board, staring at the photograph of Anton Markos that was pinned in the center. There were pen lines radiating out in a star shape, linking Markos to photographs of Alice Logan, Kerry Green and Finbar Clusky, a box containing the words CHILDREN OF HECATE? and another containing the word STRASSER.

"Does it make any sense to you, Gill?"

"No. You?"

"Not at all. Where's DS Bartlett?"

"He and Brian have gone to pick up Clusky. They should be back soon."

"Let me know when they get here. I'll be in my office."

She walked into her office, set her coffee cup down on the desk and picked up the phone. The phone on the other end of the line seemed to ring forever until an answer machine kicked in. She hated answer machines. When the beep sounded, she said, "Er, hello, Harry. It's Susan...Sue. I just wanted to thank you again for last night. Er...perhaps I can return the favor sometime. Er...well, yes. Call me sometime. Bye."

She put the phone down and swore at herself, furious.

"I sound like a bloody fifteen-year-old," she said to the empty room. The worse thing was that she felt like a fifteen-year-old.

She had sworn off men since her marriage failed twelve years ago, and coped very nicely, thank you, without a partner or boyfriend cluttering up her life. Telling herself she was married to the job and actively chasing promotion sustained her during the dark times post divorce and for the years afterwards.

But for some reason, a rumpled Romeo entered her life and turned it on its head without making much effort to do so.

"It must be me," she said. She was perimenopausal. Perhaps that was it. A sudden rush of hormones to the head.

She pulled her electronic cigarette from her bag, took two puffs and dropped it back. She wanted a *real* cigarette. "Well, if he can go without a drink, I can live without smoking," she said.

There was a tap at the door and Gillian stuck her head into the room.

"They're back. No Clusky though."

Great, Susan thought. One day it would be nice if things went according to plan.

"No sign of him, guv," Bartlett said. "His neighbor says he hasn't seen Clusky or his bike for a couple of days. He rides a red Suzuki. Normally he leaves it chained up outside the flats. It's not there now."

"Okay, Jake. Put out an APB out on him. We need to talk to Mr. Clusky. What about his mate, Terry What's-his-name?"

"Terry Butler. He says he hasn't seen Clusky in weeks. He's lying through his teeth. His girlfriend, Tracy Salmon, said that Terry told her he'd seen Clusky the night before last, and Clusky had given him the cold shoulder."

"Have another word with him, Jake. See if you can't persuade him to change his lying ways. Can the girl give us anything else?"

"I doubt it. She seems like a nice kid. Scared of her own shadow. What she's doing with a maggot like Butler beats me."

"Perhaps he's got a big dick," Susan said. "Sex can be a great enticement."

Bartlett shook his head. "No. I don't think so. Talking to her, I reckon she's still a virgin."

Susan looked at him askance. "How old is she?"

"Her ID card say's she eighteen, but it's a fake. I reckon you can knock two years off that."

"A sixteen-year-old virgin, from around here? A rare bird indeed. She should be preserved in aspic. Lean on Butler. See if you can improve his memory."

"Shall I pull him in?"

"Do you know where he works?"

"Randle's in Wick Street, it's a car repair and body shop. He's an apprentice panel beater."

"Go and pay him a visit there. Make sure his boss knows who you are and why you're there. Mention Kerry Green again, loudly. It might persuade our Terry to be more forthcoming."

"Mr. Bailey? It's Richard Frost from the Mayberry Clinic. Still no news of Alice Logan, I'm afraid. I wondered if you'd had any luck tracing her."

"Not so far," Harry said.

"Shame," Frost said. "I feel responsible. After all, she was in our charge here at the clinic when she walked out."

Harry said nothing.

"About that other matter. Dr. Tayeb and Nurse Williams. The inquest is set for next Thursday, but I've been given a sneak peek at the postmortem results."

"And?"

"I'm still not sure I should be passing this on," Frost said hesitantly.

Harry was sure that Frost was *desperate* to pass it on. He wanted to share some of the responsibility.

"Would it help if I told you that the investigation into Alice Logan's disappearance is now an official matter?"

"Really?" Frost said, grabbing the lifeline Harry was offering him.

"I work for Department 18. We are a branch of the government."

"What, like MI5 or 6?"

"Something like that."

"Well then, yes. Of course I should tell you."

Harry could hear the relief in the man's voice.

"Well, Dr. Tayeb. If you remember, I said it looked like she'd swallowed her own tongue?"

"I remember."

"Well, she definitely choked that way. Her tongue shut off her airway, but the pathologist states that her tongue must have been physically forced down her throat by a third party."

"And the nurse?"

"Her brain had been liquefied: nothing in her skull but gray sludge. I've never come across anything like it in my life. It's very unsettling. I must admit this has shaken me to the core."

"Yes," Harry said. "I should imagine it has."

"You say it's official, government business. I don't suppose you can tell me what's going on."

"I'm afraid that's classified."

"Yes, yes. Need to know. I understand."

"Thank you for your indulgence, Dr. Frost. You've been most helpful. I'm sure your cooperation in this matter will be recognized. Meanwhile, if I get news of Alice Logan, I'll make sure you're informed." He rang off and sat contemplating what he had just been told. This case was turning very ugly.

Chapter Twenty-Two

Mikey Gibson ran a stall in London's Leather Lane Market, selling cheap, knockoff handbags and purses. He'd set up the stall early that morning as usual, and was now waiting patiently for the lunchtime trade: office workers and secretaries, seemingly eager to be parted from their hard-earned money in exchange for a fake Louis Vuitton or Prada accessory. He had the Smiths playing on his iPod and hummed along with *Meat Is Murder* as he adjusted his display.

"Hello, Mikey."

He looked at the speaker: a young, pretty blonde girl who stood at his stall, turning a black and silver DKNY bag over and over in her hands. Pretty and ready to part with some cash. Christmas come early. He would have rubbed his hands together in anticipation of an easy sale, but didn't want to appear too keen. She smiled at him and something registered in the back of his mind. "I know you, don't I?"

"Artemis."

He blinked and adjusted focus, pulling the buds from his ears, leaving Morrissey to croon away in the distance. "Artemis, the goddess, that's right. Gaff in Goswell Road. I remember. Artemis, how are you? You were high that night. Mind you, I was pretty bombed myself."

"I tried to save them."

"Who? Tried to save who?"

She dropped the bag back onto the stall. "The girls. I tried to save the girls, but I wasn't well. And he…well, he was too powerful. But I'm better now, and he's dead."

Mikey looked at her. "Who's dead? Erik?"

"Erik. Anton. It doesn't matter now. He's gone."

"How did he die?"

"I killed him. I had to. He would have carried on."

"Yeah, right." *Still off her trolley.* Maybe Christmas would be delayed. "Do you want to buy a bag? Maybe a nice Prada purse."

"You were cruel to me that night," she said, her eyes dancing from side to side, the October breeze blowing through her hair, making it ripple. "You all were. Cruel."

He remembered taunting her on the balcony, goading her to leap into space.

"Like I said, I was pretty bombed out myself," he said, feeling a momentary pang of guilt. "Didn't mean anything by it. Glad you're all right now."

She looked at him for what seemed an eternity, her cold blue eyes burning into his. Finally she tore her gaze away. It seemed to take a physical effort, and then she smiled. "Goodbye, Mikey," she said and started to move away.

"Yeah, goodbye. See you around." Two young women in sharp business suits were approaching the stall. Potential customers. "Ladies, how can you help me?" he called to them, flashing his best smile. They started to approach the stall.

"Mikey?"

He turned at the voice. The girl from the night in Clerkenwell was standing twenty yards away.

Alice, that was it. Alice, not Artemis. It was all coming back to him now.

She was standing stock-still in the road. One arm pointing at him, fist clenched, the other hooked behind her, and she had her head to one side, her eyes still focusing on him intently. And then the hand of her hooked arm twitched and something thudded into his chest.

A searing pain spread like a fire through his body. He looked down at the blood pouring from a hole in his Puffa jacket and then back at Alice, standing like a statue in that weird pose. Her hand twitched again and Mikey Gibson's eye exploded in a shower of blood and jelly-like liquid. He toppled forwards onto the stall, scattering the bags and purses, and dripping red over the fake Louis

Vuittons. One of the two office girls screamed; the other fainted. Alice dropped her pose and moved on through the market.

"*Ursus arctos*," McBride said, a hint of pride in his voice.

"What?" Harry said.

"I just got the results back from London Zoo on the fur sample I found in the wounds on Anton Markos's body, and they come from the species *Ursus arctos*. To you and me known as the brown bear."

"Bear? What the hell is a brown bear doing in Barking?"

"I couldn't possible speculate. Circuses can't display animals anymore, so my best guess would be an escapee from a private zoo or collector."

Harry brushed his fingers through his gray hair. "Well, I suppose that gives me food for thought," he said.

"I should have spotted it immediately," McBride said. "The size and spacing of the claw marks, and the ferocity of the assault. A classic bear attack really. You just don't expect to find results like that on a body found in Essex. Is there anything else?"

Harry paused for a moment, trying to gather his thoughts. Something was nagging at the back of his mind, something from way back that was telling him that what he was being told was not as absurd as it seemed. He gathered himself.

"Yes, Duncan, there is. Was it you who performed autopsies on a doctor and nurse from a private nursing home in Bournemouth, the Mayberry Clinic? I was down there not long after the bodies were found, and they said a Home Office pathologist was on his way down from London to do the postmortem at Bournemouth General. Was it you?"

"Ah, no, that would be Charles. Charles Turner, my number two. I was away that day, visiting my mother at a sanatorium in Dulwich. I know the case though. I had dinner with Charles at his club two nights ago, and he was very agitated about it.

"Apparently, one of the women, the doctor I think, had her tongue driven back into her throat with considerable force, ripping the frenulum, the small fold of mucous membrane extending from the floor of the mouth to the midline of the underside of the tongue. The action blocked her trachea completely. She couldn't breathe, so she suffocated."

"And the nurse?"

"Ah, she was why Charles was so agitated. He opened her skull and couldn't find a brain. Remember, the nurse had been walking and talking moments before, but all he found in the cranium was a slurry of brain matter and cerebrospinal fluid. He'd never seen anything like it before, and he can't imagine what circumstances caused it. It's a mystery that's going to live with him for quite a while, I should imagine."

"And you can't explain it?"

"No. I'm very vaguely tempted to go for the hydrostatic shock theory—a wound, especially a gunshot—that can have a catastrophic effect on another part of the body. It's a bit of a stretch. The theory is open to debate, and, if it were found to be the case, the wound would have to be pretty devastating to produce such damage to the brain. As I say, it's only a theory, and not one I've set much store by. No, I think Charles is just going to have to live with the fact he will never get an answer to it."

"Okay," Harry said.

"Are the deaths of the doctor and nurse a department matter?"

"They're connected to the case I'm working on," Harry said.

"The bear attack and the ritual killing? Good God, man. Is nothing in your life straightforward?"

"I wish it were, Duncan. Sometimes I really wish it were."

Harry hung up and called Violet. It was time to bring her up to speed.

"Do you think it's possible that Markos did have powerful psychic gifts, and used those powers to kill the doctor and nurse, making it easy for Alice to get away from the clinic to be with him?" Violet said.

"I think it's possible, yes. I've encountered worse in my time with the department. Anyway, you described him as pure evil at the very outset. You gave me the impression that Markos posed some sort of supernatural threat. It's why I took the case on. Were you deliberately misleading me?"

There was silence at the other end of the line.

"Vi?"

He heard her draw in her breath.

"Harry, I was desperate to help her. Alice, to me, is the daughter I never had. I knew I couldn't do this on my own. Even with Jason's help, I would have struggled. I'm sorry, Harry but you were my last hope."

"Forget about it," Harry said. "As it turned out, the case is very much in the department's domain."

"So where do we go from here?" she said.

"I can't answer that at the moment. I'm missing something. I feel that all the dots are there, but I just seem incapable of joining them up. I need some time to think this through. And I need to read up on a few things."

"Do you want to use my library?"

"How's your selection of books on Greek mythology?

"Fairly comprehensive."

"Okay. I'll call in later."

"You can stay for tea and cake."

"Yes," Harry said. "I'd like that."

Chapter Twenty-Three

"Pete Roberts is clean," Gillian said.

"You amaze me," Susan said.

"Not so much as an unpaid parking fine."

"Well, I never had him in the frame for Kerry Green's murder anyway. But I *am* surprised he doesn't have a sheet. He seemed the type."

"And Brian called in. Terry Butler's done a runner. Didn't show up for work this morning, and nobody seems to have any idea where he is."

"Not even his girlfriend?"

"She's at school today, so Brian hasn't been able talk to her."

"*School? Jesus!* Tell Brian to visit the school and speak to her teacher. We need to find Fin Clusky, and Butler may be our only lead."

"But first we have to find him," Gillian said.

"Yeah. Ironic, isn't it? We have him sitting here at the station, and we send him home in a squad car. The gods aren't smiling down on us at the moment."

"When do they ever?" Gillian said.

The telephone rang on Susan's desk.

"DI Tyler," she said wearily.

"This is Deputy Commissioner Mackie, Detective Inspector. Would you mind explaining to me just what the hell you think you're playing at?"

"I'm not sure I understand, sir."

"Don't you? Who do you work for, Tyler, the Met? Or Department 18?"

Oh shit, Susan thought. *I really need this today.*

Ruth Shaughnessy picked up the stick and threw it across the wasteland.

"Go on, boy. Fetch."

Skipper, her three-year-old Jack Russell terrier, barked once and scooted off to retrieve it, tongue hanging from its mouth, stumpy tail wagging excitedly. Within seconds the dog had returned. It dropped the stick at her feet and looked up at her expectantly, waiting for her to throw it again. As Ruth bent to pick it up, she saw her husband, Liam, weaving his way along the path that led to the caravan. She guessed he'd either been to the pub or, more likely, been drinking with his mates, halfway out to sea on Clacton pier.

It was a usual occurrence. Liam and his pals, all unemployed, would meet on the pier with their cans of lager, and while away the evening until they were either drunk or moved on by the police. Today he was returning early—there were still the remnants of an early autumn sun in the sky. But he was drunk nonetheless. She could tell by the way he had swerved all over the path, and how he stood there now, at the caravan's door, desperately trying to feed his key into the lock and failing dismally.

She supposed she had loved him once, when he still had brown hair, those piercing, blue Irish eyes, and something resembling a physique. What a difference twenty years could make. The Irish eyes were still blue, but cloudy now, and they often regarded her through an alcoholic haze. The hair, what was left of it, was mostly gray, and the physique had grown and softened to the point of obesity.

She would have left him if she had somewhere to go, but she didn't—her parents had disowned her shortly after she got together with Liam, and her sister was happily married to a banker and living in Cheam with boring husband and two teenage children.

Ruth was very much on her own, but at least she had Skipper. He was dependable, so long as she fed him regularly and had an abundant supply of sticks to throw.

The Children of Hecate seemed like a lifeline. She'd heard about it from Debbie. The young health visitor who was based at the doctors' practice where Ruth worked as a part-time receptionist. The way Debbie had described it, it sounded like some kind of social club: a place she could meet people and share new and, according to Debbie, exciting experiences.

When she expressed interest, Debbie was enthusiastic, saying that she would love Ruth to go along with her to one of the meetings. She would drive, Debbie said, and it was probably best she didn't tell Liam. Ruth's deadbeat husband had a reputation in town as a drunk and a troublemaker, and no one really wanted to be associated with him. Which added to Ruth's sense of isolation and her determination to strike out on her own.

Debbie drove them to Barking, where the group was meeting at a warehouse on an industrial estate.

They entered the warehouse and the blinkers dropped from Ruth's eyes. There were a number of people there, possibly twenty or more, and Ruth was struck by how quiet it was. Most of those gathered were kneeling on hassocks in front of a stone altar, and they appeared to be praying. This was not what Ruth was expecting, and her excitement and apprehension dulled immediately. It reminded her too much of the ordeal of the Sunday morning Mass her parents would drag her along to when she was a child.

She turned to Debbie, who was kneeling beside her, and expressed her concern. Debbie just smiled, leaned into her and kissed her on the mouth. Full on the mouth. A deep, lingering kiss that seemed to last forever.

During that kiss, Debbie's tongue slipped into Ruth's mouth and began exploring, roaming over her teeth, twining Ruth's tongue with hers. And while Debbie's tongue awoke passions in Ruth she had thought long buried, Debbie's hand slid under Ruth's shirt, massaging her breasts, whilst her other hand delved down between her legs, her fingers bringing her to orgasm, quickly and efficiently.

"See, I told you it would be fun," Debbie said as they finished.

Ruth picked up the stick and hurled it again and started to walk back to her caravan.

Liam called the caravan a *trailer*. His constant diet of American cop shows and films had left him with a desire to embrace a culture he saw as much more exotic than his own. And Ruth was beginning to hate him for it. His desires were unobtainable pipedreams. Instead of working to achieve them, he contented himself with drawing unemployment benefit and pissing it up the wall.

At least the nights in Barking gave her something to look forward each week. She still didn't care for the devotional side of things, but the evenings were always daring and exciting.

She stopped at the door of the caravan and called, "Skipper?" but the dog hadn't returned with the stick. She called again and scanned the landscape, looking over the wasteland, expecting to see the black-and-white head emerge from a clump of heather or nettles. But there was no sign of him.

"Don't make me come and find you," she warned.

And then she heard him yelp. From the far side of the wasteland, where a fly-tipper had dumped an old wooden-framed bed and a large pile of black plastic sacks containing who knew what. Then she heard Skipper yelp again, followed by a long, mournful wail.

The sound made her blood run cold. The idea of losing her dog was unthinkable. Skipper was her life, her reason for carrying on, and the thought of life without the irrepressible bundle of black-and-white fur was too much to bear.

She began to run, away from the caravan, back across the wasteland, calling all the while, eyes searching for any sign.

She reached the dumped bags and bed and called again, her voice softer now, less threatening. "Come on, boy. Dinner."

The black bags moved slightly, or rather, something under the bags moved slightly, making them appear as if there were things living in them.

"Skipper?" she said, and tentatively reached out her hand to pull one of the bags to one side.

It moved so fast she didn't have a chance to register surprise or to cry out.

Something brown and covered in fur erupted from the mound of rubbish bags.

Something huge, holding a limp and very dead Skipper in what she could only describe as a large paw tipped with savage claws. Blood was dripping from Skipper's body and running from the black plastic to pool on the scrubby ground.

Ruth screamed then, a long high-pitched squeal that was cut off mid note by a slashing claw that ripped through her clothes and the skin beneath, shredding her breasts. The dead dog dropped to the ground as the other claw lashed out, tearing her throat.

In the time it took for the claws to rip through her body, Ruth Shaughnessy died.

In the caravan, not two hundred yards away, Liam Shaughnessy popped the tab on yet another can of lager and chugged it back, continuing his usual evening descent into drunkenness. He wondered briefly if Ruth had prepared his supper, and spent even less time thinking where she might be. But as alcohol surged around his bloodstream, he decided that he didn't much care.

Chapter Twenty-Four

"Are you staying for tea?" Violet said when she let Harry in.

He shook his head. "Thanks for the offer, Vi. But I've got to drive to Gatwick to pick Jason up. He managed to get a transfer on his ticket. He lands at five."

"Can't he get a taxi?"

"He could, but I want to debrief him as soon as possible, and I can do that in the car. One other thing. We can take a detour to Hertfordshire on the way back. I want to go and see your sister again. I can take Jason with me. He seemed to hit it off with your nephew, Tim. He certainly got more useful information out of him than I got from your sister and that wet weekend of a husband of hers. Can you call her and arrange it? Tell her we'll be there about eight."

"I'll ring her once you've gone. Shall we go through to the library?"

"We've found Fin Clusky," Bartlett said.

Susan looked up from her desk. "Thank God for that. Are you bringing him in for questioning?"

"Can do. Do you want him *in* the body bag, or out of it?"

"Oh, please don't tell me he's dead?"

"Okay, he's not dead."

"Really?"

"No. He's dead. Had his guts ripped out and strewn across the forest floor."

"Jesus!"

"Turned up in Epping Forest an hour ago. An old lady walking her dog came across him. He's pretty messed up. The old girl has been taken to St. Margaret's

Hospital to be treated for shock."

Susan sank her head into her hands. "Just when I thought we'd been handed a break. Get down there, Jake. See what you can find out."

"Don't you want to go yourself?"

"I'd love to, but I've been grounded. Deputy Commissioner Mackie phoned me to put me in my place. Something about straying into other jurisdictions. He wants me to stay here at Waterloo Road and stop gallivanting around London and surrounding areas, stepping on people's toes. There have been complaints."

"Who grassed you up?"

"Barking CID for one. Their Chief Superintendent Blower called Mackie and told him I was interfering in an ongoing investigation, and said interference was most unwelcome. Pompous ass."

"Yeah," Bartlett said. "Blower's like that."

"You know him?"

"Yeah, we came up through the ranks together. He was a bright spark, brighter than me anyway, so they fast-tracked him. He's anally retentive. Likes to be in control of things. I should imagine that our presence at the warehouse sent him into a hissy fit."

Susan shook her head. "Mackie also said I should...how did he put it... 'curtail our current dealings with certain officers of government departments'."

"He means Harry Bailey."

"Yes."

"That's going to screw up your love life."

"There's nothing going on."

"Oh, come on, Sue. I've seen the way he looks at you. And you him for that matter."

"Harry and I get on," Susan said defensively. "Plus, working together is mutually beneficial."

"Is that what they're calling it now?" Bartlett grinned.

"Careful, Jake. Remember, you're only a sergeant. I'm still your boss."

"I'm right though, aren't I?"

"Piss off to Epping Forest," Susan said with a smile. "And bring back something I can use. We have the murder of a young girl to solve."

Bartlett threw her a salute. "Aye, ma'am. I'll do what I can."

Violet's call came through as he was driving on the M23, fifteen minutes to Gatwick Airport.

"Stephanie's agreed to see you. Eight o'clock this evening. George won't be there. He has to work late."

"Thank heavens for small mercies."

"Go easy on him, Harry. George is essentially a good man. Dull but good."

"Who put so much pressure on his daughter to reach the dizzy height of an Oxford education that he drove her away and into the arms of Anton Markos."

"You can't say that for sure."

"That's how I read the situation last time I was there. Will Tim be in?"

"I forgot to ask."

"I hope so. I think he can fill in some important background information. I got the impression from Jason that Tim was closer to Alice than anyone. Speaking with him might show me things in a different light."

"Well, eight o'clock."

"We'll be there."

Harry pulled into the airport car park. left his car and walked through to the arrivals hall. Jason's flight landed on time, but customs and passport control were working to rule because of an industrial dispute, so it was an hour before Jason West appeared at the gate. He sketched a wave at Harry and came around the barrier to join him.

"Did you bring me a gift?" Harry said.

"I've got a souvenir pine cone in my bag. Will that do?"

"It'll have to."

"We're in car park B. Come on. We're due at Stephanie Logan's house at eight."

Jason glanced at his watch. "We're cutting it fine. No time to grab a bite to eat then?"

"I got you a sandwich. Ham and mustard, okay."

"Didn't they have prawn?"

"Yes, they did. I bought two sandwiches: ham and mustard, and prawn. I don't like ham and mustard, so I ate the prawn."

"Thanks, Harry. You're a star."

"You're welcome."

"Glad I didn't bring you a gift now," Jason said.

They made it to the house in Hitchin with five minutes to spare. On the journey, Harry grilled Jason on his meetings with Karin Metz.

"Generally, how did she seem?"

"Pissed off, especially with her grandfather, Wolfgang. She blames him for everything. For driving Markos away, and for her exile in Austria. I think she genuinely loves Markos, or her *darling Erik*, as she calls him."

"How did he do it, Jason? You know girls of that age. Markos was a good ten years older than all of them, and yet he managed to seduce them to the point where he had them eating out of the palm of his hand. What was his secret? What was the trick?"

"He filled their minds with romantic stories of goddesses. He was recreating the myths of his homeland, making it seem daring and wonderful. He was a beguiling storyteller, and he convinced them he could recreate them in the image of the goddess Hecate."

"And do you think he believed it himself?"

"I think that's what he was doing all along. Looking for a vessel. Someone he could use to bring Hecate into being. That's what his cult the Children of Hecate was all about. It seemed mystical and mysterious and I'm sure that's how he sold it to his followers."

"So the sacrifice of Kerry Green was nothing but, what, window dressing?" Harry said.

"Possibly not. I think he had some kind of paranormal power, and I think he really believed he could achieve his fantasy by using the power of human sacrifice. Remember, the only sacrifice we can lay at his door is Kerry Green. I'm willing to bet there are other bodies somewhere."

"We just haven't found them yet."

"And possibly we never will."

"And you got all this from the girl, from Karin Metz?"

"From her and from reading the files Vi amassed on him."

"But I read the files and I didn't get that much from them."

"It was all there, Harry. But you had to read them with an open mind. I'm not really sure you believed in Vi when you agreed to help her."

"I'll admit, initially I was skeptical."

"And your skepticism led you to miss things that, to an open mind, were blindingly obvious."

"Are you saying that your mind is more open than mine?"

"Frankly, Harry, yes, I am. As one gets older, the mind becomes cluttered with preconceptions. They get in the way. Why do you think children can solve logic puzzles that have adults tearing their hair out for days? Younger people have the ability to think laterally. It's more natural for them. Reading those files, I was doing just that. Making jumps in logic that simply passed you by. I'm not saying my brain's better than yours, far from it. It's just…"

"Younger. Yeah. I get it." Harry yanked open the car door and got out.

"You're angry with me."

"No, I'm not, Jason. I'm angry with myself. Those books on the backseat. I borrowed them from Vi's library because there's something locked away in my mind that I can't access. It's something that I've been taught or read somewhere that's going to help me understand what is really going on here. The books are all on Greek mythology. They are going to provide the key to help me find something, some piece of knowledge that's been lost in the mists of my deteriorating mind. Age, it's a bugger."

He walked up the path of Stephanie Logan's house and rang the doorbell.

"If Tim's there, I want you to talk to him." Harry said. "Gain his trust. Get him to open up."

Chapter Twenty-Five

Stephanie Logan answered the door and led them through to the lounge. The television was on and a game show was playing. Tim Logan was slouched in a chair in front of it.

Stephanie went across to the set and switched it off.

"Hey, I was watching that," Tim complained from his chair.

"Then go and watch it in your room if it's so important. We have company."

Tim gave Harry a surly look.

Jason let the edge of a packet of Marlboro Lights protrude from his pocket and let Tim see them, then nodded towards the kitchen door. Tim got to his feet, walked out to the kitchen and opened the back door. Jason followed him.

"I'm sorry about Tim. He can be so rude," Stephanie said to Harry when they were alone.

"He's probably worried about his sister," Harry said.

"We all are, but manners cost nothing. I really don't approve of his smoking. I hope your young friend knows that."

"Better nicotine than crystal meth."

Stephanie winced. "I spoke to Violet. She tells me that awful man is dead."

"Yes," Harry said without elaboration.

"But Alice is still missing. You don't think she's..." Her voice trailed off.

"We're doing everything in our power to find her," Harry said.

"George thinks we should call the police again, but after the way they were last time, I really don't see the point. They'll just fob us off with platitudes and heavy hints that we were less than perfect parents and drove her away." A sob caught in her throat. "It's not true, Mr. Bailey. We were a happy family. That holiday in Greece, those days in the scorching sun, lying by the pool, eating out in the evening at the local tavernas, were probably some of the happiest times of my life. And Alice loved every moment with us. We felt so close to her, and she said she felt the same about us. Even Tim enjoyed it. He wasn't rude to us once. He and Alice took themselves down to the beach every day. It was like it used to be when they were small, and George and I would take them to Clacton. I used to lie by the pool and imagine them having all kinds of adventures."

Her voice trailed off again as she lost herself in her memories. Harry sat there, saying nothing, but wondering if Jason was faring any better.

"When I was here last," Jason said, lighting the cigarette he'd given Tim. "You said you'd know if Alice were dead. How can you be so sure?"

"I just would."

Jason remained silent, waiting for him to elaborate.

Tim smoked and stared down the length of the garden. It was mostly lawn and the rust-colored remnants of what was once a colorful display back in the summer.

"Auntie Vi told us you used to work for her."

"Still do, on occasion."

"Then you'll know Alice is a witch, like Gran. She was a witch too. I don't know how Mum got away with it, but she's totally straight. The closest she gets to witchcraft is listening to Harry Potter audio books, and she only does that because she has a thing for Stephen Fry."

He dropped the cigarette to the ground and looked to Jason. Jason offered him another and lit it for him.

"Alice and I must have inherited the gene from Auntie Vi, Alice more than me. I get feelings and the occasional premonition, especially when Stevenage are playing. Our local soccer team," he added by way of explanation.

"Yeah, I guessed."

"But Alice, she inherited the lot from Vi. Seeing auras, a sixth sense, moving things with her mind without touching them. A whole lot of freaky stuff."

"Did it bother you?"

"No, it was great. She was a sensation at parties. She could bend spoons—not the gimmicky conjuring trick that Uri Geller did. She could really bend them— tie them into knots just by holding them between her thumb and forefinger. No rubbing or stroking the metal. She'd just hold the spoon and stare at it, and the bloody thing would curl up like a pretzel. Other kids used to come to the house just to watch her, at first. Then I think she started to freak them out, so they stopped coming."

"When I came last time, you described her as being as mad as a box of frogs. What did you mean by that? I asked you at the time but you wouldn't tell me."

"Yeah, well, I was seriously pissed of with Dad that night. He'd been going about his *precious Alice*. How butter wouldn't melt. He drove her away, smothering her. She worked like fuck to get to uni, not so much that she wanted to go, she just wanted to get away from him."

"So mad, how?"

"Come back inside and I'll show you." He led Jason back through the kitchen and up two flights of stairs, to the top floor of the town house.

"In here," Tim said, opening the door at the top of the stairs wide and ushering Jason inside. He followed him in. "Alice's bedroom," he announced.

Jason stood in the middle of the room and let his gaze sweep over the place. A single divan bed; a wardrobe, so full the doors would not close fully; a dressing table littered with tubes and bottles of makeup; a hairbrush and dryer; a set of ceramic hair-straighteners; a box of tissues. It was a typical teenage girl's bedroom—nothing to set it apart.

And then he looked at the countless pictures and posters covering every inch of the wall and made a quick reevaluation. No pop idols of the day, no pinups from teen magazines. Instead, the walls were covered by posters and pages torn from books, each image a representation of a god from Greek mythology: Apollo rubbing shoulders with Athena, Hera fighting Hermes for wall space.

Above the bed, the wall was covered by one poster, a depiction of a beautiful woman with long, flowing hair, set against a night sky, glowingly lit by a huge crescent moon.

The woman held a bow and arrow, bowstring pulled back and taut, the wickedly pointed arrow aimed at an unseen target. The poster dominated the room, reducing all the other images to supporting characters in this Greek drama.

"Artemis," Tim said, noting where Jason's attention was focused. "Goddess of the hunt and wild animals. Alice claimed her as her own, identified with her totally. It became something of an obsession for her."

"When did it start?"

"When we were kids. Someone gave her a picture book filled with images of the gods—a strange thing to give a kid—and she became obsessed with it. She was never interested in Barbie or My Little Pony, but give her a cheap toy bow and arrow and she became Artemis. She'd play for hours, lost in her own little world. As she got older, the books she was given by my parents…hell…by everybody, just reinforced her obsession. Eventually her interest in Greek mythology started to take over her life. Mum and Dad encouraged her to channel her preoccupation into her schoolwork. It was why she worked so hard to get to Oxford. As I said, she wanted to get away from Dad, but if she was going to uni, she was going to get the best classical education that the system could provide. And there is nowhere better for that sort of thing than Oxford or Cambridge. Nothing second best for our Alice. Dad nearly wet his pants with pride and excitement when she was accepted for Oxford. He basked in her reflected glory for months. It didn't matter to him that his little girl was leaving home."

"It mattered to you though."

"I knew I'd miss her and my life would never be the same again." He laughed, suddenly and bitterly. "She used to call me Apollo. Apollo was Artemis's twin brother, so that fitted in *her* mind. 'Hey, Apollo, let's go and play.' She'd grab her toy bow and arrow and she'd be off, and I'd follow. Mostly to the park, but when we both got our bikes we'd cycle over to Letchworth and play on Norton Common. It's a bit wilder over there."

"What kind of games would you play?"

"Hunting, mostly. I'd go and hide and she'd hunt me down and shoot me with her bow and arrow."

"Didn't it hurt?"

Tim laughed again, a happier laugh this time as he remembered the game. "No. It was only a toy bow. The arrows had rubber section cups on the end of them, not points. But she got bloody good with it. She could get me from the most impossible angles. She told me that when she got to Oxford, she joined their archery club, started winning competitions and stuff. She was a natural."

"But mad."

"Oh, totally bonkers…but in a good way." Tim stopped and stared down at the floor. "You *will* find her, won't you? I really miss her."

He had tears in his eyes.

"I'll certainly do my best," Jason said.

"Thanks."

"Could you show me Alice's room?" Harry said.

"Why on earth do you want to see her room?" Stephanie said, slight panic in her voice.

"I'm trying to build a clearer picture of your daughter. Seeing her room would help."

Stephanie got to his feet. "Well, if you think it will help."

"It will. Truly."

"Then you'd better come with me."

Harry followed Stephanie out to the hall and up the stairs.

As they reached the first floor landing, they stopped as they heard voices coming from above their heads. Stephanie ran up the next flight of stairs two at a time. "Alice? Alice?" She froze in the doorway at the top of the stairs.

"Tim," Stephanie said with anger in her voice. "What are you doing in Alice's room? It's her private space." Harry was a few paces behind her on the stairs.

"Well, she's not here to complain, is she?"

Jason stepped forward. "My fault, Mrs. Logan. I wanted to see it...for the same reason as Harry, I should think."

Stephanie turned to Harry, a question in her eyes.

Harry was nodding. "I trust Jason's instincts," Harry said and, when Stephanie turned back to her son, winked at Jason.

"Very well," Stephanie said. "Anything you think might help you in bringing Alice home. I'll leave you to it. Please try to leave the room as you found it." She turned on her heel. "Tim, downstairs with me." She moved past Harry and started to descend, Tim close behind her.

"Phew, she's—"

Harry put his fingers to his lips. "We'll talk in the car," he said and walked across the room to get a better look at the pictures on the far wall. "This reminds me of Markos's apartment in Clerkenwell," he said. "Some of these pictures look like they've been torn from the pages of an encyclopedia of Greek mythology."

Jason nodded to an overfilled bookcase in the corner. "Well, she had enough to choose from," he said, but Harry wasn't listening.

He was staring at the picture of Artemis affixed to the wall above Alice's bed. "That's it," he mumbled. "How could I have missed it?" He turned to Jason. "Come on. I've seen enough," he said, and then stalked from the room and padded down the stairs.

Chapter Twenty-Six

"Are you still here?" Bartlett said as he walked into Susan's office.

"No," she said tiredly. "I went home two hours ago. This is a mirage."

"Like that, is it?"

She nodded. "Have you been at Epping all this time?"

"Yes," Bartlett said. "Things went a bit sideways."

"But it *was* Clusky?"

"Oh, yes. It was Clusky all right. It's the other two they can't identify."

Susan leaned forward in her seat. "*The other two?*"

Bartlett pulled up a chair and sat down. "Two young women, stabbed with a star-shaped knife. Buried in shallow graves not six feet from where Clusky was found."

Susan shook her head incredulously. "What's going on here, Jake?"

"I don't know," he said. "I saw McBride when I was there, and he's scratching his head too. Did you know he thinks Markos was attacked by a bear?"

"No," Susan said. "Barking CID have shut me out. It's their case now, and they're not sharing information... *A bear?*" It suddenly sank in what Jake Bartlett had just said.

"That's right." He pulled out his notebook. "*Ursus arctos* to be precise. A brown bear."

"And how did the professor arrive at that conclusion?" Susan said.

"From the claw marks and fur found on Markos's body."

"I don't believe it," Susan said.

"It gets better," Bartlett said. "He reckons Clusky was killed by a bear too."

"The same one?"

Bartlett shut the notebook and put it away. "The odds against having one bear roaming through Essex are pretty high," he said. "What odds would you give for *two* bears going on a killing spree?"

"Pretty astronomical."

"Yeah, that's what McBride said. He's going to DNA test the fur to see if it came from the same animal."

"And what about the girls?"

"McBride thinks it's the same killer who killed Kerry Green. The stab wounds are identical. A five-bladed knife thrust through the aorta. Death would have been almost instantaneous."

"Anything else?"

"Both had a crescent-shaped carving on their abdomens and both had a coin placed under their tongues."

Susan yawned. It had been a long day and she was all in.

"You should get some sleep," Bartlett said.

"What would be nice," Susan said, "would be to go to sleep tonight and wake up in the morning to a new, different reality, because this one's shitty."

"Never going to happen," Bartlett said.

"More's the pity."

"Well, that's me done. I'm going home. My little girl, Willow, is three, and she's starting to think her father is the boy who delivers the papers. She sees more of him than me."

"Good night, Jake."

"Night, guv."

Susan waved him away and dialed Harry's number. It went straight to answer machine. "Hi Harry, it's me again. Don't worry; I'm not stalking you. I'm not turning into a bunny boiler, but I really need to talk to you. Two more bodies have turned up with the same MO as Kerry Green. Call me on my cell when you get this message. It doesn't matter how late. Bye." She stood and grabbed her coat from the stand and left the station.

Within minutes she was walking in through her front door.

She had just closed it behind her when her phone sounded from the pocket of her coat.

"Hi."

"Hi, Harry," she said.

"Sorry, I've only just got in and heard your messages. What's this about two more bodies?"

"Hold on," she said, carried the phone through to the kitchen, took a can from the fridge, popped the tab and returned to the lounge. She collapsed onto the couch and kicked off her shoes. "Right. You're not going to believe this," she said, and proceeded to tell Harry about the truly bizarre day she'd had.

"This case is beginning to fry my brain," she said. "It's going into meltdown. And my boss doesn't want us working together."

"If it's any consolation, I was hauled over the coals by Crozier today for the same reason. Your deputy commissioner has been a busy boy."

"He called him too? Christ!"

"Calm down. Crozier can get the Home Secretary to have a word in his ear. Get him off our backs."

"That's all right for you, Harry, but it will fuck my career. I'll get a reputation for being a troublemaker. I know what Mackie's like. He holds grudges."

"Then what do you suggest?"

"We carry on as we are, but we don't visit crime scenes together. We'll speak on our cell phones and keep each other up-to-date."

"Does that mean we can't see each other?"

"I don't know. I'm making this up as I go along. I've never been in this situation before. This bloody thing is spiraling out of control. *Bears!* It was bad enough with devil worship and satanic cults. Now we have bears going around killing our suspects. Where's it going to end?"

"I'm working on a solution."

"Well, good luck with that. Let me know if you find one. I'll raise the flags."

Harry could understand her frustration. He'd worked cases where nothing made any sense, and seemed to go round and round in circles, and he didn't have to worry about someone further up the chain of command scrutinizing his every move and weighing up his future career prospects. Crozier could be a pain in the backside sometimes, but he always played fair and let his investigators use their own initiative when it came to handling a case. Susan had a hierarchy of senior officers and yards of red tape to overcome.

"Look," he said. "It's late. I'm tired. You're tired. Let's talk about this tomorrow."

She sighed. "You're right," she said. "I just needed to vent. Sorry you were in the line of fire. Good night, Harry."

"Good night, Sue. And we will get together for that coffee. Sooner rather than later, okay?"

"Okay," she said, and hung up.

Harry stared at the phone and shook his head, dropping it onto the couch next to him. Then he pulled one of the mythology books from the pile Vi had lent him, opened it and started to read.

He was still reading three hours later. It was all coming together in his mind. Things were starting to make sense.

He looked at the clock. The numbers read 2.31. He closed the book he was reading and went to bed.

"We've got someone interesting in interview room one," Bartlett said as Susan walked into the station the next morning.

"If you've arrested Winnie-the-Pooh, Jake, I don't want to know."

Bartlett smiled. "How about Terry Butler? He walked in this morning, claiming that someone's out to kill him."

"Oh, this should be interesting," she said.

"Right, Terry," she said. "What's going on?"

Butler was distraught. His eyes were wide and he kept glancing behind him "I've seen her," he said. "Watching me. First Mikey, then Fin—she probably had something to do with Davy falling under the Tube train."

"You're babbling, Terry. Take a breath, calm down and start from the beginning."

Twenty minutes later they were still sitting there. "So this girl you met at the flat in Clerkenwell, who nearly threw herself off the balcony, does she have a name?"

"She called herself Arty-something."

"And you saw her again, you say, yesterday?"

"She was outside in the street. I've been staying at a friend's squat. It's a big empty house in Clapton. I saw her through the window, just standing there, staring up at the place."

"Did you speak with her?"

"No, I hid. I knew about Davy and Mikey and I'd just heard about Fin. That's the four of us who were there that night. Three of them dead, and I'm next."

"And her name's Arty. You're sure?"

Butler nodded, swallowed noisily and licked his lips.

"And whose flat was it?"

"A bloke called Strasser. He's a mate of Fin's."

Susan exchanged looks with Bartlett.

"Well, thank you for bringing this to our attention, Terry. We'll look into and be in touch. Where can we reach you?"

"And that's it. That's all you're going to do about it?"

"As I said. We'll look into it."

"How the fuck does that help me?" He'd pushed himself out of his chair and was leaning across the table angrily. Jake Bartlett was out of his seat in an instant, and placed a restraining hand on Butler's shoulder, guiding him back down to his seat.

"You don't understand. You're not listening to me. She's going to kill me, just like she killed the others."

Susan stood up and walked to the door without a word. Bartlett followed her out of the room. In the hallway, Bartlett said, "What are we going to do with him?"

"Let him sit there for a while to calm down, and send him on his way."

"Is that all? What about Fin's friend, Strasser? That's Markos, right? Shouldn't we check it out?"

"Yes, of course we should, but we can't," Susan snapped at him. "The Anton Markos case is no longer ours. Barking CID is dealing with it, and I've been told, in no uncertain terms, to keep my nose out of it or face disciplinary charges."

"But the girl was probably Alice Logan."

"Yes, it probably was, but I've been told to stay away from that too. My hands have been tied with red tape. All we can do is concentrate on Kerry Green's murder and matters arising from that."

Jake Bartlett stared at her. He was shaking his head.

"What else do you expect me to do, Jake?" she said hotly. "The only reason we wanted to speak with Butler was in the hope he'd lead us to Fin Clusky. He comes in here, bleating that someone, who could be Alice Logan, is going to kill him, but what evidence has he given us? Sweet FA, that's what. Davy Coltrane was hit by a train, Fin Clusky was disemboweled by a bear—if you believe Professor Mackie—and I haven't even heard of Mikey Gibson."

"Do you want me to check him out?"

"Yeah, check out Gibson, but send Terry Butler on his way. We can't be wasting time with this."

"Very well," Bartlett said.

"No, wait," she said. "My hands might be tied but there's no reason I can't refer him somewhere else. Hold him a bit longer while I make some calls."

Susan walked back to her office and slammed the door. Sometimes she felt like crying out of sheer frustration. This was one of those times. It got worse when after a few calls she was left with no alternative but to let Butler go.

Chapter Twenty-Seven

Bastards! They weren't listening to him. Terry Butler walked away from Waterloo Road police station, hoodie pulled up to cover his head, his eyes dancing from side to side, watching the street. Why didn't they believe him? He had seen her through the window, standing outside the squat. He'd ducked back out of sight, but he was sure she'd spotted him.

He'd go away, away from London. He had an aunt in Braintree. He didn't like her and she didn't like him, but she was his mother's sister and was really into families pulling together in times of crisis. And this was a crisis.

He took a right into Lombard Street and stopped dead. The blonde girl was there, standing at the end of the street: standing and staring at him, holding her arm out in front of her, as if pointing at him, but her fist was clenched. His instinct was to turn and run, but his legs were paralyzed. "What do you want from me?" he yelled.

There was no one on the street he could turn to for help. He simply stood rooted to the spot and stared back at the girl. Alice, not Arty. That was her name. *Alice.*

He'd call out to her again—try to reason with her. Tell her that what happened that night wasn't his fault. It was Fin. He was to blame. He opened his mouth, but the words never reached his lips. The girl moved her other arm behind her, opened her fingers, and something hit him in the chest, burning a hole straight through it, making the back of his jacket explode in a crimson shower.

Butler fell forward onto his face, breaking his nose on the tarmac, not that it mattered. He died a few seconds later.

"Hi, Maria. It's Harry."

"Hello," Maria Bridge said.

"How's life treating you in Edinburgh?"

"Fine, Harry, just fine. Look, I really have to get to the hospital in a moment."

"Yeah, sure. I won't keep you. I know you have a busy life."

Up until six months ago, Harry had been in a relationship with Maria. She'd been the doctor who had treated Crozier after his attack. The relationship ended when Maria said she'd had enough of living in London and working at a busy metropolitan hospital and decided to move away. The fact that she'd gone to live in Edinburgh and work at one of the busiest hospital in Scotland suggested to Harry that it was him and not London she'd had enough of.

"Look," she said. "I meant to call you but…well, you know what it's like. When we were together, our work was always an issue. Scheduling times when we could be together was—"

"Stop, Maria. I didn't call you to discuss our relationship. I respect your decision to leave London. Let's leave it at that, okay?"

"Okay. Then why did you call?"

"I need some information about crystal meth addiction."

"Are you sure you've called the right person? I'm a surgeon. I take out peoples' appendixes, repair people when they injure themselves. If you want to talk about drug addiction, you'd be better off talking to a counselor."

"And I'd get a load of mumbo jumbo about social causes, psychological issues, and the reason why they're taking it in the first place. I need to talk to someone who's been at the sharp end, who has seen addicts on meth highs, without being lectured about how they got there. I figured, with the time you put in at the accident and emergency department of a busy London hospital, you would have dealt with junkies doing just that, not looking for a referral to rehab. What can you tell me?"

"Methamphetamine is a psychostimulant that can induce a state of euphoria, increase libido and heighten concentration, among other things. Those are the plus points. On the downside, it can cause irritability, aggressiveness and excessive feelings of power and grandiosity."

"So if you believe you're an immortal, crystal meth will fuel that belief?"

"Oh, yes. It can turn a control freak into a megalomaniac and lead some anonymous bureaucrat to believe they're Napoleon Bonaparte. I saw both in my time at St. Thomas's. The most dangerous issue here, though, is when the user is tweaking or bingeing, they can suffer from hallucinations so vivid that they seem real, and disconnect from reality. Then they can become a danger to themselves and others."

"Well, that's all I wanted to know really. You've been very helpful."

"You're welcome. Look, Harry, I wish things had turned out differently. I didn't want to hurt you."

"It's life, Maria. It happens to all of us. Maybe I should have handled things differently, but we'll never know. Look me up if you come down to London."

"I don't suppose you have much call to travel to Edinburgh."

"No, not a lot."

"Well. If you do…"

"Yeah, I know where you work. Thanks for your help, Maria," he said and rang off.

"She's hunting," Harry said to Jason and McKinley. "She's not Alice Logan anymore, not in *her* head. She's Artemis, the hunter."

Jason stared at him. "What are you talking about, Harry?" he said.

They were in Harry's office, Jason seated across the desk from Harry. McKinley was sitting to one side, watching Harry with rapt attention. "So who's she hunting, Harry?"

"Anyone who crosses her path and tries to hurt her, and those she's sworn to protect."

"This is making no sense, Harry," Jason said.

"No, it didn't to me until last night. I saw Alice's bedroom, and I went home and gave myself a refresher course on Greek mythology. And earlier I spoke to someone who knows about the effects of the crystal meth that Markos got her addicted to. I think Alice now believes she's Artemis, something she's played at being in the past. The drug has twisted her mind and caused her to lose all sense of reality."

"So is that all we're dealing with here?" McKinley said. "A junkie?"

"If only it were that simple," Harry said.

"I've just come up with something on Mikey Gibson," Bartlett said as he walked into Susan's office.

"And?"

"He was killed yesterday in Leather Lane."

"That's the market, right?"

"Yeah, he had a stall there."

Susan closed her eyes. "How was he killed?"

"Wounds to the chest and eye. We're waiting for the lab report to establish cause of death."

"Any witnesses?"

"Two women, one of whom fainted. We're questioning them now. And another stallholder, a Mr. Ali Khan, says Gibson was on his stall as usual, talking to a potential customer. She went, and a minute later Gibson keeled over onto his stall. Khan said it looked like he'd been shot, but Khan didn't hear anything to suggest that was the case. No gunfire, nothing. One minute he was standing there, and then there was blood on his clothes, and then his eyeball ruptured."

Susan drummed her fingers on the desk. "Did Khan give a description of the potential customer Gibson was talking to just before he died?"

"Female. Young, pretty and blonde."

"Shit!" Susan said. "Get Butler back in."

"Too late." Gillian said from the doorway. "Terry Butler has just been found dead in Lombard Street. Miriam Jackley's been called. She's on her way there now."

Susan looked at Bartlett. "I know, Jake. I know."

"Tell John what you told me last night when we left the Logans', Jason."

Jason stood up and started pacing the room. "Alice Logan seems to have paranormal powers, inherited from her aunt, Violet. Tim Logan describes Vi Bulmer as a witch, but I've seen her in action. She's not a witch per se but she does have some very well-developed psychic powers: clairvoyance, ESP, psychometry, precognition, telekinesis... You name it, Vi has it."

"Which, if Alice has inherited half of the powers Vi has, makes her very dangerous indeed."

"And if she's inherited all of Vi's powers?" McKinley said.

"Then we're in trouble," Harry said.

"So what about the bear?" Jason said. "Psychic powers don't explain the bear attacking Markos."

"That brings us back to Greek mythology," Harry said. "The closest relation of the name Artemis in Greek is *árktos*—bear, and according to mythology, a cult arose around Artemis, probably a survival of some ancient totemic and shamanistic rituals that would have formed part of a larger bear cult found further afield in other Indo-European cultures. Did you know that the bear is one of the oldest European deities?" Harry stopped talking and flipped open a book on his desk and ran his finger down the page.

"Artemis also turned her handmaidens into bears and made them dance for her, and she herself has been depicted in bear form."

"Christ, Alice has gone all the way in her delusions, hasn't she?" McKinley said.

"But Harry," Jason said, "all this is *mythology*. It doesn't explain the bear that attacked Markos. That was real, very real."

"It doesn't make sense to me...yet. But there has to be an explanation," Harry said. "A bear? In Epping Forest?"

"Maybe she's a shape-shifter as well?" Jason said.

Harry shook his head. "Unlikely. It doesn't fit with the myth, so I'm keeping an open mind about that one," he said. "I know shape-shifters exist, because I've dealt with one before, but I don't think Alice is a shape-shifter. What it means, though, is that we need to keep our wits about us, and—"

"So, what's your take on Anton Markos now?" Jason said. "Do you still think he was responsible for the deaths of the doctor and nurse at the Mayberry Clinic?"

"I think Anton Markos had some limited psychic power, but basically he was a charlatan," Harry said. "A smooth talker, able to bend young women to his will and make them act out of character. But ultimately he was a sad, deluded man who dedicated his life to bringing his fantasy, his passion for a picture, into reality. He wanted to reestablish the goddess Hecate here on earth. Drugging the women he desired, using human sacrifice and whatever means he thought would help him achieve his goal. Ironic really. He tried to reestablish Hecate on earth, and got Artemis instead. And his folly killed him." He looked steadily at Jason. "We say nothing to Vi about this until we're sure."

"This is going to break her heart, Harry."

"I know it will," Harry said grimly.

Chapter Twenty-Eight

"DI Tyler."

"Susan?"

"Harry, can this wait? I'm up to my eyes at the moment."

"I won't keep you," Harry said. "I just needed to tell you. The emphasis on finding Alice Logan has shifted. We now suspect she was instrumental in Anton Markos's death."

"And how long have you waited to tell me this?"

"Minutes. I've only just finished putting it all together in my head."

"Well, I'm ahead of you, Harry. We now have an all points out across London to find and apprehend Alice Logan."

"Why the change?"

"We believe she might be responsible for the deaths of Mikey Gibson and Terry Butler, and possibly two others."

"Who are they?"

"Those two, together with Fin Clusky and Davy Coltrane, were all at Anton Markos's apartment when Alice was there. There was some kind of incident with Alice on the balcony. She was as high as a kite. They were all goading her and taking the piss. Now they're all dead, the latest being Butler, who was killed minutes after we interviewed him. Though how she knew he was here is anyone's guess."

"She's hunting them down, Sue, and wiping them out. She believes she's Artemis, Greek goddess of the hunt."

"I don't believe this," Susan breathed into the phone. Louder, she said, "Why and how?"

Harry gave her a concise version of his theory. "Basically, she's destroying anyone she believes is mocking her or potentially hurting her. It's why I think she killed Markos. He got her hooked on drugs and he was using her. Fin Clusky too, if she thought Markos was getting the drugs from him."

"And the two girls who were buried where we found Clusky?"

"No. I think you can lay those squarely at Markos's door. It was probably Clusky who disposed of the bodies, which explains *where* he was killed. Alice wasn't responsible for them, or Kerry Green for that matter. Their bodies all had crescents carved into them postmortem. The crescent is the symbol for Artemis, and all three girls had coins placed under their tongues to pay for their journey across the River Styx. Alice was trying to ease their passage to the other side. Artemis, in legend, was also the protector of young women. She was doing what she saw as her duty by them."

"This is all totally whacked out," Susan said. "I've got a drug-fueled psycho, who believes she's some sort of goddess, with paranormal powers and a huge chip on her shoulder. That's one for *Crimewatch*."

"It doesn't end there, Susan,"

"What do you mean?"

"The Children of Hecate. They were all complicit in the sacrifice of the girls. How many hassocks did they recover from the warehouse?"

"I don't know. Barking police have shut me out of the investigation. I don't have access to that information, but I would say fifteen, possibly twenty."

"Then we have fifteen or possibly twenty more victims. She's going to try and hunt them all down and kill them."

Susan sat back in her seat. "Shit," she said. "But we don't know who they are."

"No...but Alice does," Harry said.

BBC News London.

A bright-eyed young woman appeared on the screen, standing roadside.

Behind her, trees and greenery.

"And finally: police in Essex today cordoned off certain areas here at Epping Forest, after a man was reportedly attacked by a *bear*."

She was trying hard not to smile and pressed on regardless. "A police spokesman said they were treating the threat as 'credible'."

The screen switched and a policeman in a crisp and very smart police uniform, complete with peaked cap, appeared on the screen against the backdrop of a large glass building bearing the legend *Essex Constabulary*, written in blue letters on a cream-colored board. The red bar at the bottom of the screen read, *Chief Constable Edward Marr, Essex Police.*

"At the moment we are treating this report as credible, and we would ask the public to avoid the cordoned-off areas of the forest, and to help their local police by reporting anything they see that they would consider to be unusual. While we don't think there's any immediate threat to the public, we would ask for their vigilance and ask them to keep clear of the forest until we have completed our inquiries. Thank you."

The screen switched and bright-eyes was back. "Earlier, we spoke to Mike Preston, bear-keeper at Colchester Zoo."

What followed was a two-minute talking heads piece, dragging in comments from experts on bear behavior.

Back to bright-eyes. "I think the message is, don't go down to the woods today, as you could well be in for a big surprise." She smiled at the last comment, obviously pleased with herself for managing to get her quip into the broadcast. "Sasha Lancaster, BBC News, Epping Forest."

Harry's phone rang. "Have you seen the news?" Jason said.

"I've just watched it. A four-minute fluff piece at the end of the broadcast, in the *humorous stories* spot. I don't think they're taking it seriously."

"I agree, but how else could they have handled it without causing panic? I thought the policeman got the tone just about right. Panic is the last thing the police need just now. In all honesty, there's no real threat to the general public. Alice is targeting specific victims. I don't see her as a danger to anyone else. Mind you, if I were a member of the Children of Hecate, and knew what was going on, I'd be shitting myself."

"I suppose you're right," Jason said, a shade begrudgingly. "What are we supposed to do? Sit back and do nothing?"

"Pretty much. I doubt they'll find anything, and if they do, Susan Tyler will hear, and she'll call me."

"So we sit and wait for Alice to make her next move?"

"As I see it, Jason, we don't have any choice. At the moment, Alice is in the wind. She could be anywhere. We have to wait for her to show herself again."

"And in the meantime, someone else is going to die."

"I know," Harry said. "I know."

By the dim light of his sitting room desk lamp, James Chesterton sat at his PC, trawling through Internet sites, looking for some club, some group to fill the hole in his life that, until recently, had been filled by the Children of Hecate. Not that he was ever a believer, and some of the rituals, especially the kneeling and the chanting, were a bit of a pain, but the naked girls on the altar, the knife and the blood, well… Not even the porn sites he frequented on the Internet could give him that kind of rush.

Chesterton was thirty-two, unmarried, and still lived with his aging parents. He occupied the back part of the house: two rooms overlooking the garden. One room was a bedroom with a pine bed, a wardrobe, a chair and very little else. One wall was given over to *Star Wars* wallpaper, very old and fading slightly, but that didn't matter. Color pinups from lads' mags and "top shelf" periodicals were stuck to the wall, and hid the fact that C-3PO was looking a little tarnished and Chewbacca looked like he was molting.

The other room was what he called his bachelor pad. From the black velvet drapes to the red leather Ikea couch, he liked to think of it as his seduction room. The unpalatable truth was that, on the rare occasion he found a girl to come back to his place with him, she was turned off either by his bookcases filled with

Star Wars and *Doctor Who* action figures, or by his mother, usually wearing her nightdress, who would bustle into his room unannounced to see if Johnny or his "friend" would like a "nice cup of tea".

He had just opened a page on sci-fi collectables when something tapped lightly on one of the glass panels of the French doors. The house was large. His elderly father was the vicar at St. Bede's Presbyterian Church, a hundred yards up the hill, and the house was the vicarage attached to it, where the family lived on Reverend Chesterton's stipend and the small amount of cash James brought home from his job at the local Halfords.

He spun round at the sound at the doors, his pulse rising slightly. He thought it might be Thea, a rather plain girl with mousy, usually unwashed hair who worked at the fish shop in town, who had promised him she would come round to see him one day.

He got up from the computer and cupped his hand to peer out at the darkened garden. He squinted. He could just about make out the rounded shape of the box hedges his mother so lovingly trimmed, the ornamental concrete birdbath, and the stand of five apple trees at the bottom, but not much else.

Blaming his imagination, he pushed away from the doors and went back to his computer. Before he could refresh the screen, he heard another sound. This one was like a fingernail being drawn down a chalkboard. He sprang up from his seat again and went to investigate, unlocking the French doors and yanking them open.

He stepped out into the night, pulling his woolen cardigan tight around him to ward off the chill, and someone whispered his name.

"James."

It seemed to come from the area of the garden where his father grew vegetables. He looked intently but couldn't see anything, but then he heard a sound, a kind of shuffling, the sound a hairbrush being drawn over coconut matting would make.

"Is anybody there? Thea, is that you?" he hissed, and glanced back into the room to make sure his mother hadn't come to investigate.

"James." Another whisper.

He took three steps onto the crazy-paved path, and had almost reached the greenhouse when something reared up from the vegetable plot.

Huge, with long dark fur, the bear towered above James. It opened its mouth and gave an ear-splitting roar that seemed to rattle his head and caused his bladder to open and expel its contents down his leg, soaking his pants. The bear raised its long claw-sharp arm and brought it slashing down, tearing James's face from his skull. It slashed again and opened up his chest to the rib cage, several of the claws catching in his ribs and ripping them out of his chest.

With a mewling cry, Chesterton fell to the path and died a few seconds later.

Chapter Twenty-Nine

"So far," Harry said, "there have been three bear attacks and one attack that appeared to be a gunshot wound, but was actually made by, McBride thinks now, an arrow. But lack of any kind of residue in the wound has him scratching his head. All he will say is that the holes are about three-eighths of an inch in diameter, and they pass through the entire body, piercing the heart."

"Yeah," Susan said. "He told me the same thing. Frankly, Harry, I'm not sure what to do next. It's been three days since the last attack and since then, nothing. I was expecting a bloodbath, but it just hasn't worked out like that. The bear attacks were a fifty-year-old man from Dagenham who was walking his dog in the local park, a middle-aged woman from a caravan park in Clacton, and a vicar's son from Billericay who was attacked in the back garden of the vicarage and had his face torn off and his chest ripped open."

"What did Essex police do?"

"From what I picked up on the grapevine, they widened their search to the area involved and found nothing. They've called off the bear hunt after complaints from local shops and street traders that the police presence and closure of the forest were having an adverse effect on business. I saw on the news this morning that they've reopened the forest to the public."

"Are they still freezing you out?"

"Oh yes. They think they can solve all this without the help from other areas. Bloody idiots! No fresh leads at your end?"

"No. Nothing. Alice seems to have dropped off the planet."

"Well, she must be somewhere, doing something."

"Yes, she must be. I phoned my doctor friend again, and she seems to think that Alice could be suffering from what she called 'meth crash'. It happens when the body shuts down, unable to cope with the drug effects overwhelming it. It results in a long period of sleep for the person that can last one to three days. So it could be why she's stopped killing."

"Like a bear hibernating... But where do you think she could be? Also, where's she getting the meth from now Markos is dead? She must have a supplier."

"All questions that have been running through my mind...and I haven't been able to answer one of them."

"So we're going to have to wait for her to make the next move."

"It looks like it."

"Bloody frustrating."

"But good news for potential victims."

"True."

"How about that drink?"

"I was thinking about that too. Tonight?"

"Yeah, fine."

"Same time, same place. You bring the dominos."

He laughed. "Yeah, I'll do that. See you then."

The line went dead on the sound of her laughter.

Violet was lying on the deeply cushioned couch in the sitting room of her Chelsea home, with her eyes closed.

The room was large, with a high ceiling and ochre-painted walls. The furniture was eclectic, collected from the many places she had traveled. Middle-Eastern carpets clashed with Moroccan wall hangings. Ethnic-styled furniture in *sheersham* and reclaimed oak gave the room a rustic, slightly African feel. A teak root mirror hung from the wall over an authentic cast-iron, art nouveau fireplace original to the house.

Candles covered every surface, and incense sticks smoldered in their hand-beaten brass holders, filling the room with the heady scent of sandalwood. The effect of the incense and candlelight combined to make her feel drowsy and allow her mind to drift—exactly the state she wanted to achieve.

She found it relatively easy to reach a trance state without resorting to drink and drugs; the teachings of a swami in Bengal had helped her harness her own astral body and allow it to roam free, while she lay there and absorbed all the images and sensations it experienced.

Now, as she relaxed, her breathing slow and rhythmic, she stretched out her thoughts, searching for her niece—searching for Alice, out there in the ether.

Once it been no problem connecting to her, but since Alice had started using drugs, Violet had found the pathways closed to her, and her niece's mind an enigma shrouded in mystery and perplexity.

Today she prayed she would finally make a connection with her.

As she lay there, her eyelids fluttered and her eyeballs danced beneath them. Soon images were filling her head, sweeping her away to another place, another dimension.

She was in a field, a lush green space of verdant grass and crimson poppies. A roe deer traversed the space, stopping occasionally to chew the grass, before looking up with startled eyes and gamboling off to stop at another part of the field. In the distance she could hear the discordant baying of a pack of dogs, close by, lost somewhere in the trees beyond the field.

The scene shifted and she was walking through a forest of densely packed ash and elder, the forest floor beneath her a carpet of autumn-shed leaves and bark and twigs stripped and snapped from the surrounding trees. She sniffed the air and smelled something that reminded her of wet copper. Her prey was near, almost within touching distance. The odor of blood grew stronger as she picked her way through thickets of nettles and thorns, her legs protected by the thick brown fur that covered them.

She saw him then, sheltering close to a swathe of rhododendrons, his eyes frightened, sweat beading his body, his smell a palpable, cloying stench. On his arm was a crude image of Hecate's wheel, drawn in ink, a labyrinth contained within an outer circle, and she knew without any doubt the he was the one.

She approached him, a low growl rumbling deep in her throat, the stink of his fear almost unbearable. She was a yard away from him and he was holding out his hands to protect himself, but they were nothing but a flimsy barrier, no match for her claws, claws that swooped through the air, rending and tearing, ripping the skin from his body, the flesh from his bones. Blood spurted from ruined, torn arteries and painted the trees a glorious crimson, dripping down the ragged bark and forming pools of scarlet liquid on the forest floor.

"Oh, dear Lord!"

Violet's eyes snapped open and she jerked upright. The sensation she had just experienced bewildered her for a moment, but the clouds of confusion gradually parted and she started see the awful, horrible reality.

"Alice, my precious Alice. What have you become?" And then a searing pain coursed through her chest, and she clutched at it with desperate hands, willing it to pass, to leave her in peace, but the pain only increased, tightening like a metal strap around her heart and lungs. She gasped once and fell unconscious back on the couch, spittle dribbling from her lips as her skin slowly turned from pink to blue.

Jason let himself into the Chelsea house with his own key. He shut the door behind him and stood in the quarry-tiled hallway, calling her name. "Vi? Vi, it's me. Where are you?"

There was no reply, but he sensed her presence in the sitting room, ran to the panel door and pulled it open. She had collapsed there, half on and half off of the couch. Her skin gradually turning bluish gray, cyanosis setting in as her body was starved of oxygen.

He yanked his phone from his pocket and called for an ambulance, then crouched down beside her and rested his fingers on her throat, feeling for a pulse. It was there, thin and weak, and close to, he could see her chest rising and falling almost imperceptibly. He stroked a lock of russet hair away from her face and held her close to his chest as tears started to trickle down his cheeks.

"Don't you die on me, Violet Bulmer. Don't you die on me, you silly cow." Away in the distance he could hear the mournful wail of the ambulance approaching. "Soon," he whispered, as he rocked her gently in his arms. "They'll be here soon. And then you'll be all right."

After what seemed a lifetime, there was a single ring of the doorbell. He laid her gently back down on the couch and went to open the door to the paramedics.

"I'm thinking of handing in my papers," Susan said.

"Leaving the force?" Harry said, surprise registering in his eyes.

"Pretty much."

They were sitting in the same booth they had shared before at the Wellington. Paul Anka was crooning from the jukebox: "Diana".

"But why?" Harry said. "I had you pegged as a career copper."

"Perhaps that's why. So did I." She sipped her spritzer. "Twenty-five years with the force and all I've achieved is detective inspector. It's too late for me to climb any higher. I can quit on full pension."

"What, and spend the rest of your life raising begonias and watching daytime TV?"

"I may have loftier ambitions than that. I used to picture myself on the Algarve, running a bar. Sun, sea and sangria."

"Sangria's Spanish. The Algarve's Portugal."

"Thanks for the geography lesson, but I knew that. They still serve sangria though."

"Why now, Sue?"

"Truth be told, the Anton Markos case," she said.

"I'm sure you've handled worse in the past."

"It's true, I have, and I don't mind blowing my own trumpet here. I've handled them pretty damned well. That was why it was so galling to be booted off the case by that asshole Mackie. He's paper pusher, a very highly paid one. He knows nothing about real detection. He couldn't find his prick in a dark room if it didn't have luminous paint on it."

"And does it?"

"What?"

"Have luminous paint on it?"

She shuddered. "Pray to God I never have occasion to find out...but you know what I mean. Take Jake Bartlett. Married, two kids, still living in a police flat in Shoreditch, not pulling in a quarter of Mackie's salary, and Jake's ten times the copper than Mackie will ever be."

"So it's all down to pay grades and pecking orders. Is that why you want to quit?"

"I'm forty-five," she said. "Married once, disastrously, no kids to look after me when I'm old and gray, working umpteen hours a day, going home and snatching a ready-meal, then going to bed to sleep for perhaps five hours before getting up and doing it all again. I feel like I'm living in a permanent loop of hard work for precious little reward."

"Not even job satisfaction?"

"So, what, we catch the buggers, only for some mealy-mouthed, overpaid judge to let them off with a slapped wrist. I'm beginning to think, is it all worth it?"

"This is beginning to sound an awful lot like self-pity to me." Harry said.

"Well, fuck you, Mr. Bailey," she said, but her face broke into a smile. "Get me another drink, before I forget I'm a lady and smack you in the chops."

He smiled back her, picked up her glass and took it to the bar for a refill.

As he was standing there, waiting for the barman to finish with another customer, his phone rang in his pocket.

When he got back to the booth, Susan said, "What is it, Harry? You look like you've seen a ghost."

"That was Jason on the phone. Vi Bulmer's had a heart attack. They've taken her to the Chelsea and Westminster Hospital and put her on life support. I'm going to have to go over there."

"I'll drive you," she said.

"Thanks, but no, I couldn't put you out..."

She had her coat on before he had even finished the sentence.

"I'm happy to wait around as long as it takes. Come on," she said. "Let's go."

Chapter Thirty

They arrived at the hospital and found their way to the intensive care unit.

A nurse sat at a desk at the end of the corridor, surrounded by a bank of monitors where she could keep an ongoing check on her patients' condition. Harry approached the desk. The nurse, a dark-haired girl with large, expressive eyes, looked up at him and smiled. "May I help you?" she said, an Irish lilt to her voice.

"I'm here for Violet Bulmer," he said.

The nurse picked up a clipboard and consulted it. "IC5," she said. "Just up there on the left."

"Thank you," Harry said.

"Just two visitors at the bedside," the nurse said.

"It's just the two of us."

"Yes, but Ms. Bulmer already has one visitor."

"It's okay, Harry. I'll wait here," Susan said, and crossed to one of the two seats against the wall and sat down.

"There's coffee there," the nurse said to her, nodding to a silver vending machine farther along the corridor. Susan smiled her thanks. Harry walked along and found IC5.

He could see Vi through the large, square window. She lay on her back, her head propped up on a pillow, a clear oxygen mask covering her nose and mouth, and an array of wires snaking from different parts of her body, connected to a vital signs machine. Harry was hurled back in time eighteen months, when he had visited an ICU at a different hospital to see his boss and friend Crozier after Simon was attacked and left for dead on the Embankment, next the River Thames.

Another year and another friend, lying in a hospital bed, fighting for their life.

Jason sat at her bedside, looking ashen, his curly black hair awry, cheeks streaked with tears.

Harry entered the room. "How is she?" he said

Jason had his gaze fixed on Violet's sallow face. "Not good," he said. "The doctor said she's had a major coronary. It was lucky I went round to her house when I did. Another half an hour or less and she would have died."

Harry sat down on the other chair at the bedside. "Can she hear me?"

"She shows no sign that she can. I came with her in the ambulance, and she hasn't acknowledged my presence yet. The doctor wants her kept quiet."

"What's the prognosis?"

"Too early to tell, but he did say that given her age and her condition, she should make a complete recovery."

"I've never known her ill before. I know she was in hospital earlier in the year, from injuries sustained during your abortive investigation, but I've never known her *ill*."

Jason chuckled. "No. Vi's a tough old bird. Her energy levels put me to shame and she has fifteen years on me."

"How did you two meet?" Harry said.

"She used to be a volunteer prison visitor, and she would come and see me in Wandsworth."

Harry's eyebrows rose slightly. "What were you in for? If you don't mind me asking."

"I was a naughty boy back then. Nothing serious. Stealing cars, a spot of housebreaking. Nothing violent. Vi came to visit me once as part of her volunteer work, and kept coming back."

Jason continued to stare at Violet, but behind his eyes, he'd drifted back in his mind. "She'd visit and we'd sit there and talk for hours. I told her about the psychic experiences I'd had since childhood, and she shared some of hers. We had a connection. She helped me out when I was released. My parents had chucked me out and I had nowhere to go. Vi let me stay at her house until I'd got myself back on my feet. I found a job in a pub, bar work, that came with a flat above the pub. I did that and lived there until she asked me to provide backup on a case she was working on. I quit the pub and I've worked for her off and on ever since. I suppose you could say she took me under her wing."

"You two seem very close."

"She means more to me than my own mother," Jason said, and Harry saw the tears start to well again in his eyes.

Harry reached across the bed and laid a reassuring hand on his arm. "She'll get over this, Jason. She'll pull through."

"Yeah," Jason said. "As I said, she's a tough old bird."

"Not so much of the old."

They both turned to look at Vi, whose eyes were half-open and staring at them.

"Good to have you back, Vi," Harry said.

Jason made a sound in his throat, somewhere between a cheer and a sob, and held on to her hand tightly.

"It's all right, Jason. I'm not dead yet." Her voice was weak, no more than a whispered croak, and he had to lean forward to hear her clearly. "It'll take more than a heart attack to make me shuffle off this mortal coil," she said, and gave a small laugh.

The Irish nurse bustled into the room. She had obviously been keeping a close eye on Violet's progress. "If you gentlemen could wait outside," she said and pulled a thermometer from her tunic and slipped it under Vi's tongue.

"What do you think she was doing to bring this on?" Harry said when they got outside the room.

"When I got to the house, I found her in the sitting room. She had lit candles everywhere and incense sticks burning, so I should imagine she was roaming."

"Roaming?"

"She has her own technique for freeing her astral self and letting it wander, searching for things and going to places that would be impossible to get to in her corporeal state."

"What do you think she was searching for?" Harry said.

"I would have thought that was obvious. We still haven't found Alice yet, and it's been over three weeks since she went missing."

"I wonder if she found her."

"The fact that she's lying there now in intensive care, wired up to a heart monitor and other things, I would say yes, she probably did. Or came close."

"Shall I take you back to the Wellington, or do you want to go home?" Harry said as he and Susan drove out of the hospital car park.

"My car's parked at Waterloo Road," she said. "You can take me back there and—"

"Sorry the evening's been such a bust," Harry said, interrupting her.

"I was going to say, you can take me back to the station to pick up my car and then you can follow me back to my flat. You can come in for a nightcap."

"But I don't drink," Harry said.

"Then I'll make you coffee. Or is it cocoa for you geriatrics?"

"Cheeky cow," Harry said with a smile.

Susan let them in to the flat. It was on the first floor of a purpose-built block on Swan Street. "Excuse the mess," she said, leading him inside.

Harry looked around the cluttered lounge, at the stacks of magazines, piles of CDs and a desk that held an old iMac and piles of household bills and fliers for local takeouts. There was an open can of Red Bull next to the computer, sitting on a CD she was using as a coaster.

She moved a pile of official-looking papers from the seat of a brown, cloth-covered couch and dropped it on the floor.

"Take a seat and I'll put the kettle on." She walked out to a small kitchenette and Harry heard the kettle being filled. She put her head back through the doorway. "Coffee?"

"Please." Harry said, pulled a copy of *Police* magazine stacked in a pile by the window, and flicked it open.

Susan came back into the living room a short while later, carrying two steaming mugs of coffee. "Black, no sugar," she said. "Instant, I'm afraid. I hope that's okay."

"It's what I drink at home."

She sat down next to him on the couch, leaned across and kissed him on the lips. Harry put his hand behind her head and pulled her closer. "I've never kissed a police officer before," he said when they broke the embrace.

"How was it?" she said.

"Hmm. Arresting."

"Oh, please."

Their lovemaking ebbed and flowed, torrid and gentle in equal measure, but always passionate. Susan had a slender body, with firm breasts and a tight, flat stomach, and Harry took great pleasure exploring every inch of it with his hands and tongue. When he slid his hand down the smooth, flat expanse of her belly and through the neat bush of her pubic hair, she opened her legs slightly and moaned softly as his fingers probed the moistness.

"Not bad," she said when they were spent. "For an old man."

He slapped her playfully on the buttocks. "Not bad yourself," he said and lay there looking up at the hairline cracks on the ceiling, listening as her breathing changed into something deeper and more rhythmic, and he realized she was asleep. He pulled the duvet up to cover her shoulders, then rolled over. He was asleep within seconds.

He awoke suddenly, disoriented, trying to grasp where he was, then felt Susan move slightly beside him and remembered. He slid his legs from the bed and padded across to the window.

It had rained and the road below was slick, reflecting the orange light from the overhead street lamps. Somewhere a cat yowled and another answered it. A dark van moved slowly along before turning the corner at the end and disappearing from view.

She was out there somewhere. Alice, the self-styled goddess, with a murderous streak. Lips brushed his neck. He hadn't heard Susan rise and cross the floor to where he stood.

"Can't sleep?" she said.

"I can't switch my brain off," he said "I drift off and have visions of Vi, in her hospital bed, with Alice standing over her holding a five-bladed knife, and then I wake up.|"

"Drink," she said with a yawn. Her normally sleek bobbed hair was ruffled and astray, and she'd pulled on a tartan robe that was at least three times too large for her, swamping her slight frame. She looked younger, smaller and adorable.

"Do you have any tea? Coffee won't help the insomnia."

"Sure thing," she said, pecked him on the lips and went out to the kitchen.

When she came back with the cups, he was still standing, gazing out through the window.

"What are you thinking?"

"I'm thinking I owe it to Vi to find her niece."

"You *have* tried. We all have." She took her tea across to the bed and sat, crossing her legs under her and pulling her robe down to cover her knees. "I don't see what else we can do. We have half the Met out there looking for her, and her photo's been circulated to other forces throughout the country. I wouldn't say it's a full-scale manhunt, but it's pretty damned close."

"I appreciate all your help with this," he said.

"No problem," she said. "Come back to bed."

He took one final look along the street and joined her on the bed, where they drank their tea and made love again, before falling asleep until the buzzing of Harry's cell phone awakened them a few hours later.

Chapter Thirty-One

"Mr. Bailey, it's George Logan. I'm sorry to call you so early, but Violet's in hospital, and I really didn't know who else to call." There was note of hysteria in his voice.

Before Harry could respond, George continued. "It's Tim. He's been arrested. They've taken him to Hitchin police station. They have him in a cell. They've locked him up, Mr. Bailey."

He sounded at the end of his tether.

"Why?" Harry said calmly.

"Possession of a class A drug."

"Shit," Harry said under his breath. "Did the police give you any idea what drug it was?"

"Methamphetamine," George said, his voice suddenly cold. "That was the drug that bastard Strasser got Alice hooked on." And then he started to cry. Huge, racking sobs that traveled down the phone line and made Harry feel sick and slightly useless.

He should have seen this coming. Alice was still out there, alone. She was an addict, and she'd have the need to feed that addiction, and who better to help her in that quest than her loyal and loving twin brother? Her Apollo.

"Who was that?" Susan said, concerned at the anguish that had settled over Harry's face and the deep lines of concern etched into his brow.

"George Logan. Hitchin police have arrested Tim, his son and Alice's twin brother. I'm going to have to get over there."

"I'll come too," Susan said.

"Haven't you got to go to work?"

"It's my day off. I'll come. I might be able to help. We'll just shower and go," she said.

"Thank you," Harry said.

"No problem. You'd do the same for me."

He looked at her steadily and felt a surge of affection flow through him. Yes, he probably would.

They took his car. Harry drove up the A1 while Susan made some phone calls.

"Possession with intent to supply," she said. "He must have had a lot of the stuff on him."

It had started to rain again, and the wipers were working hard to clear the rain and spray from the windscreen.

"It wasn't for him," he said. "It was for Alice."

"How can you be sure?" Susan said.

"I've met him. He shows no sign of being a user. A cigarette smoker maybe, but no drugs, I'm sure."

"Then if it's for Alice, he knows…"

"He knows where she is. Yes, that's what I was thinking."

Harry left Susan talking to the desk sergeant while a uniformed PC led him to an interview room on the first floor. Tim was sitting there at a table, a plastic cup of water in front of him. He looked terrified. The PC followed him into the room and closed the door, taking up a position beside it.

Harry had used his Department 18 identity card to get him this meeting, and having Susan Tyler with him hadn't done any harm either, He was grateful she was with him. Her presence oiled wheels that would have otherwise been slow to turn.

Harry sat down at the table and stared across it at Tim Logan, who was looking at anything in the room apart from him. Harry sat back in the chair, crossed his arms—crossed his legs. "Where is she, Tim?"

Tim stared down at the desk.

Harry sat forward and rested his elbows on the table. "Tim, look at me. Where is Alice?"

Tim gradually dragged his gaze up to meet Harry's. The fear was still in his eyes, but there was something else as well. Defiance.

"I don't know what you're talking about."

Harry had to keep his anger in check. He spoke quietly but firmly. "I'm talking about your sister who you used to play with when you were children. I know the meth was for her."

"It's mine," Tim said.

"And we both know that's total bollocks. I'll bet you've never taken anything like it in your life. You've probably enjoyed the odd spliff or two at parties and suchlike. But crystal meth? No. I don't believe it. It's in a different league. Why don't you give yourself a break and tell me the truth?"

"It's mine," Tim said again.

Harry shook his head. "Tim, you had enough methamphetamine on you to keep most of the junkies in Hertfordshire going for a month. Where did you get the money to pay for it?"

"I paid for it. I have a job."

"In a burger bar, yeah, slapping ground beef onto a griddle for minimum wage. You're earning barely enough to keep your motorbike on the road, let alone buy this amount of gear…is that what you call it, gear?"

Tim looked at him blandly and shrugged.

"Who's your supplier?"

"Some bloke."

"Does he have a name, this bloke?"

"I don't know. I met him in a pub. The Horseshoes. I didn't ask."

Harry sighed, loudly, and sat back. "You're full of shit," he said. "You didn't get a name because there was no bloke."

"Where did I get it from then?"

"I don't know, Tim. Where *did* you get it from?"

"You're so bloody clever. You tell me."

"Where's Alice, Tim?"

"I don't know what you're talking about."

Harry stood up. The room was small and windowless, and there was a single radiator, spewing out dry, sleep-inducing heat. Harry's armpits were growing damp. He walked from the room and stood outside to take a breather.

This was going nowhere. He wished he'd brought Jason with him. Jason was more of an age with Tim, and had built a rapport with him. But Jason had other things on his mind. Violet for one.

"Harry."

Harry turned and Susan was walking along the corridor towards him. At her side was a man, thin-faced, with black, wavy hair and piercing blue eyes. He was about Susan's age.

"This is Detective Inspector Frank Ryman. He might be able to help."

Harry stuck his hand out and the two men shook. "Tim Logan. He's the brother of the missing girl, Alice, right?" Ryman said.

"Yes, he is."

"According to Susan, she's a meth addict, and you believe Tim got the drug for her and might know where she is."

"I've just questioned him and didn't get anything out of him."

"I tried earlier to get some answers from him regarding his possession, but I drew a blank too. I was considering releasing him on police bail and putting a tail on him. I'm thinking now that we could kill two birds with one stone here. We want to find his supplier; you want to find the girl. If we put him under twenty-four-hour surveillance, then it's only a matter of time before he leads us to, if not one, then both of them. I understand that his sister's being looked at as a murder suspect."

"Yes," Harry said. "I'm afraid she is."

"Then using the manpower is justified."

"I think it's a good plan," Harry said. "So, yes, I'd say it's justified."

"Good, only I have to square it with my superintendent. Costs are one of his hobbyhorses. He watches us like hawks to see we don't waste public money. Sometimes it's like trying to police with one arm tied behind our backs. Can I liaise with you, Sue?"

"Sure," she said, and gave him her contact card. He looked at the card and put it in his shirt pocket. "Great. I'll set the wheels in motion," he said, and leaned forward and kissed her cheek. "Lovely to see you again," he said. "Mr. Bailey." He nodded at Harry, turned and retraced his steps.

"Won't involving another force get you in trouble with Mackie?" he said.

"Probably. But you know, I'm past caring. I meant what I said last night about quitting the force. If we find Alice and stop all these killings, at least I'll go out with a bang and not a whimper. Do you think it's worth having another go at Tim?"

"No. I won't get any more from him. He's protecting his sister," Harry said. "Let's leave it to Ryman to execute his plan. Let's go back to London. We could have lunch."

"Yes," she said. "I think I'd like that."

"Have you worked with DI Ryman before?"

"No," Susan said.

"Only you two seem quite familiar."

"I know his wife, Annie. She's a JP. We've sat on a number of committees together, and I've had dinner at their place a few times. That's how I know Frank."

"Ah, I see."

"Frank's a good copper and hates the politics of the job as much as I do."

"It's good to have him on our side."

"Yes," she said, turning to walk back along the corridor. "Yes, it is."

Harry stood there, and then followed her.

Jason was waiting for Harry in his office when he arrived in Whitehall the next day.

"Hi, Jason," he said. "How's Vi?"

"She continues to amaze and confound doctors with her recovery rate," Jason said with a smile. "I told you she was tough. It's probably too early to say this, but it wouldn't surprise me if she were up and around in a couple of days."

"That's great news," Harry said and brought Jason up-to-date with what had happened at Hitchin police station yesterday.

"But that's fantastic," Jason said. "It gives us our first hard lead to find Alice. Do you think it might work?"

"You spoke to Tim Logan. Did he seem like a drug user to you?"

Jason shook his head. "No. Despite giving his parents a hard time, and his 'rebel without a cause' stance, I think Tim's straight as a die."

"That's why I think he's going to be conflicted. He's helping his sister out of loyalty, even though he knows it's fundamentally wrong to do so. I think in the end, it will be their downfall. Anyway, why are you here? Shouldn't you be keeping Vi company?"

"No," Jason said. "The last thing she wants is me moping around her and watching that she doesn't exert herself. She told me to go away and make myself useful somewhere else. But actually I thought I'd come and tell you to stop worrying about telling her the truth about Alice. She knows."

"Did you tell her?"

"I didn't have to. I was right when I said she'd been roaming yesterday. She actually connected with Alice at last. Vi's been trying and failing to reach her since she took off with Markos."

"Did she get any clue of her whereabouts?"

"No, but she was inside her mind when Alice killed again last night. She didn't give me all the details, but I gather it was pretty gruesome. I think it was the nature of the killing that brought on the coronary. Now Vi's impatient to get back to her library. She said she wanted to read up on a few things."

"She didn't show any signs that she was upset about Alice's true nature?"

"Quite the reverse. I think she partly blames herself for the way Alice is. She seemed cold, like ice. She said, 'This is down to me, Jason, and it's up to me to fix it'."

"And what did she mean by that?"

"I don't know. But she had that steely look in her eye. I've seen it before when she means business. I wouldn't want to get on the wrong side of her when she gets like that."

Chapter Thirty-Two

Sarah Palmer had worked hard all morning. Hamish Anderson, her boss, had been on her back since she came in at eight. "File this, Sarah," "Call them, Sarah." *Yes, sir, yes, sir, three bags bloody full, sir!*

She stepped out onto the balcony that ran the length of the building, and took a pack of cigarettes from her bag, slid one out and lit it. Not being able to smoke inside buildings was stupid. Didn't the legislators understand that people who smoked often did it to relieve stress? And working for a pig like Hamish Anderson was the cause of her stress.

Sarah was forty-six, unmarried, with a son who was now in his late twenties and who lived in Canada with a wife and children. She hadn't seen him in over ten years, and had never seen her grandchildren.

For a while, earlier this year, she had thought life was starting to get exciting again. Like it was when she was in her teens. She'd met a man, Wade, who had shown her that life could be fun after forty. They had started a passionate relationship, based on nothing other than sex, and that sex had been the most daring she had ever experienced. He'd introduced her to bondage, S&M, fetishism, and awakened something in her that she'd always suspected was there, but had always denied.

When he told her he was taking her somewhere special, somewhere that would take her to new levels of erotic fulfillment, she had jumped at it. But when they arrived at a warehouse on a bleak industrial park in Barking, she'd struggled to maintain her enthusiasm. Not very shades of…

When they got inside though, she had to revise her opinion. The lights were low and there were at least twenty people in there, men and women, all in states of partial undress. Wade was snatched away from her by a young woman with long, raven hair, wearing a leather thong and very little else. Sarah panicked at first, being left on her own. But she wasn't on her own for long. A man, a similar age to herself, but well muscled and very good-looking, appeared at her side, started to whisper in her ear, made suggestions to her that were so forthright and so graphic she could feel herself blush.

But as he continued to whisper his obscene litany of things he was going to do to her, she started to become aroused and made no protest when he peeled the clothes from her body. On a coarse blanket on the floor of the warehouse, she had sex with him. Let her body be used in ways she could have only imagined in her sickest, most twisted fantasies.

When the sex was done, and the people in the warehouse were exhausted, spent, lights at the side of the warehouse came on. Twin spotlights illuminated a stone altar. A naked girl with short dark hair was lying on the altar, her hands and legs restrained, a band around her head to stop her twisting it to see the anticipation of the people in the room, many of them kneeling on small, rectangular cushions, lips opening and closing in silent prayer. All of them with their attention fixed on the altar.

At first Sarah though this was the prelude to some communal sex game, perhaps an orgy of some kind, and her pulse started to quicken.

When the handsome man wearing a long, scarlet robe appeared at the rear of the altar with a beautiful, young, blonde girl at his side, Sarah was convinced she was going to witness something she had never seen before. The man in the robe started speaking, intoning the words like a priest giving a sermon in church. Foreign words she didn't understand. The young blonde woman stared straight ahead, eyes blank, unseeing, as if her mind was lost on a private voyage to some distant place. She was not connecting to events happening around her.

When the man took the strange-looking knife from his robe, his congregation gasped. When he lifted the knife and plunged it through the chest of the young dark-haired girl, a cry went around the room, almost exultation.

Sarah didn't witness the events that followed. She quickly gathered up her clothes, dragged some of them on, rushed from the warehouse and threw up.

Wade found her outside a short while afterwards. He seemed intoxicated, high. She let him guide her to the car and drive her home. When she reached her house, she got out of the car and ran inside, swearing to herself that she would never see him again.

So now she found herself smoking a cigarette in the chilly October air, standing on the balcony of the office building that Hamish Anderson and Associates occupied. Bored, desperately bored of her life and wondering if she should contact Wade again.

She took a step towards the rail to launch her cigarette stub into space, and saw a young woman staring up at her from the car park. The woman was wearing a short, white tunic dress, made from a thin material that caught in the October breeze.

She must be freezing, Sarah thought, but the girl didn't seem affected by the cold. She stood there, staring up at Sarah, her left arm extended. And, in that instant, Sarah recognized her as the blonde girl from the warehouse.

"Hey!" she called, but as the words left her lips and were whipped away by the wind, the girl drew back her other arm in a quick, fluid moment and splayed her fingers.

Sarah was thrown backwards by the force of something driving through her chest. It drove her against the glass and she was suspended there for a moment, before her knees gave way and she slid down the window, leaving a bloody slug trail on the glass.

For a moment Sarah Palmer just sat there, wondering why the front of her blouse had turned from white to red, and why she seemed to have a hole in her chest. And then a savage, electric pain coursed through her. Her head fell forward and darkness engulfed her.

It had been a slow start to his shift at the burger bar in the Stevenage retail park. His manager had him cleaning tables with an antibacterial spray and a roll of paper towels. When the girl wearing the uniform of the local school—plaid skirt, green sweater over a white blouse—came through the double swing doors, Tim

Logan was back behind the counter. He smiled at the girl wearing the uniform and said, "What can I get you?"

"Cheeseburger and large fries, with a chocolate shake," she said. She wore her curly ginger hair short and had retainers on her teeth, but she had nice eyes.

He took her money and handed her the change. "Fries will be a couple of minutes. Take a seat and I'll bring it over to you."

The girl thanked him and took a seat at a table in the center of the restaurant to wait for her meal. She had chosen a table with the remains of someone else's meal cluttering a quarter of it. Tim watched her as she moved the detritus to one side, pulled a schoolbook from a schoolbag with a One Direction decal covering one side. She glanced back at him and smiled.

A few moments later, the bell on the fryer rang, and Tim went across with a brown paper bag and started to assemble her order. He glanced across at her, caught her eye and smiled at her again. He opened the bag, dropped in two twenty-pound notes at the bottom, measured the fries into a thin cardboard container with an aluminum scoop and placed it in the bag, then went back to the burger delivery slide and picked up the paper-wrapped cheeseburger, placing it in the bag, next to the fries and on top of the banknotes.

The shake machine had been playing up since he'd arrived earlier, and it took an age to fill the paper cup. Finally the hose dribbled to a stop, and he snapped on the lid. He pulled a tray from the pile at the side and laid it on the counter in front of him. He placed the bag and the shake on it, threw on two napkins and a red-and-white plastic straw and carried the whole lot across to the girl, who had her schoolbook open on the table in front of her.

He placed the tray down beside her, took a discarded tray from an adjacent table and started to load the remnants of the previous customer's meal onto it. The girl wearing the retainers on her teeth flashed him another metallic smile and nodded down at the small grip-seal bag of crystal meth lying in the center of her open schoolbook.

As Tim cleared the rubbish, he glanced about to see he wasn't being observed, scooped up the bag of meth and dropped it into the pocket of his tunic. Then he took the tray across to the waste bin and pushed open the hinged front, slid the contents of the tray into the plastic sack below and returned to the counter. A few minutes later, the ginger-haired girl had finished her cheeseburger and fries, taken the money from the paper bag and hidden it in her schoolbook, which she closed and placed into her One Direction satchel. She looked across at him one last time, smiled again and left the burger bar, still sucking on her chocolate shake.

Detective Constables Bob Mason and Ken Perkins from Hitchin CID sat in their car on the west side of the Stevenage retail park and watched the burger bar where Tim Logan had spent the past four hours working his shift behind the counter.

Mason fidgeted uncomfortably in his seat. "Something's happening. They're shutting up for the night." As they watched, the lights went out behind the counter and the front door opened. Tim Logan walked out and continued around the side of the small, square building to where he'd left his trail bike.

The two DCs heard the bike start with a tinny roar, and then Tim rode across the car park towards the exit.

"Go," said Mason as Perkins started the black Mondeo. "Don't let him out of your sight."

They followed, closely but not close enough to be seen. "He's heading towards the A1," Perkins said

"And home, I expect," Mason agreed. "Another wasted night."

They crossed three of the town's many roundabouts, keeping Tim's taillights in view. "Probably," Mason said. But at the next roundabout Tim took the left-hand exit.

"This isn't the way," Perkins said.

"Just keep on him. Let's see where he's taking us."

They followed but hung back, the distance just about allowing them to see his taillights. "Pull in a little closer," Mason said. "Don't, whatever you do, lose him, or Ryman will have our nuts for breakfast."

The road gave onto a narrow lane, cutting across woodland. Perkins sped up and slowed down to negotiate the bends in the road.

They turned the next corner.

"Where did he go?" Mason said.

Perkins switched the headlamps to full beam to scan the road. Either side of the lane were dense stands of trees.

Tim sat on his bike, headlamps switched off, hidden from view between the tightly packed sycamore and ash, and watched the unmarked police car drive past slowly, the driver's and his passenger's necks craned forward, looking for any sign of his trail bike. He was smiling. He'd seen them watching the burger bar earlier when he'd gone out for a smoke, but they obviously hadn't realized he'd spotted them.

"Follow me now, idiots," he said, turned the bike on a sixpence and sped off through the wood.

"What do you mean, they lost him?" Susan barked down the phone. "I thought your men were up to this. He's only a kid, Frank, not Steve McQueen."

"His motorcycle was the off-road type," Ryman said, acutely embarrassed. "He probably took off across country. We'll just have to visit the Logan house and wait for him. If he has more meth on him, we'll find it."

"And if he's not gone to restock his stash and has gone to see his sister instead, where does that leave us?"

"With egg all over our faces."

"Precisely."

"Sorry, Sue."

"Not your fault, Frank," she said wearily. "Just call me if he turns up."

"Will do."

Susan hung up the phone, slamming it down on its cradle. "Sod it!" she said, and then picked up the phone again and rang Harry to give him the bad news.

Chapter Thirty-Three

The house had been empty for years. Buried deep in the middle of Burwell Wood, it had been home to squatters and vagrants and a colony of wild dogs. Now it had reached such a level of disrepair and dereliction, they had all moved out and moved on—even the dogs.

Tim pulled aside the sheet of corrugated iron that covered the entrance and slipped inside, switching on his Maglite and sweeping it across the floor. Most of the boards had rotted, and one wrong step would mean a ten-foot drop to the cellar below.

The stairs were just as rotted and just as treacherous. He kept to the edge of the treads and picked his way up, holding tightly on to the mold- and lichen-covered handrail. "Ally," he called softly. "I'm here."

He made his way along the landing to the room and stepped inside. She was crouched in a corner of the room, the sleeping bag he had brought a few days ago wrapped snugly around her body. He shone the flashlight over her, and she shielded her eyes with her hand.

"Apollo," she said softly. "I knew you'd come."

"Yeah, Ally, I'm here," Tim said. "I'll always be here for you."

"I know," she said. "I know."

"Some good news at last," Harry said. "Jason just called. Vi's out of intensive care. She's been moved to a private room."

"That's great, Harry," Susan said into the phone. "I wish *I* had some for you. Frank Ryman phoned me earlier to tell me that Tim Logan didn't return home last night. He hasn't been seen since they lost him in the lanes last night."

"So now we have both Logan children missing. Great."

"And there was another killing yesterday afternoon in Stevenage. A woman called Sarah Palmer was killed at her place of work. The preliminary report from McBride suggests she suffered similar wounds as Terry Butler and Mikey Gibson. Stab wounds to the heart made by a long, thin, cylindrical object—possibly an arrow, McBride's thinking now, but one that leaves no trace evidence in the wound. And Scene of Crime hasn't produced any evidence to support his theory. No arrows have been found at the crime scenes."

"Nor are they likely to be," Harry said.

"What do you mean by that?"

"I'll explain it to you, but it's going to require you keep an open mind," he said.

"Harry, since I met you and got to learn about Department 18, my mind's been opened in ways I couldn't have imagined a few years ago. Let's hear your explanation."

"Okay," Harry said. "I've been up all night thinking this through. Vi Bulmer has some pretty amazing paranormal powers. I've seen her in action and know that to be the case. I think some, if not all, of those powers have been passed down to Alice through the bloodline.

"Did you know, when she was a child, she used to bend spoons for the amusement of other kids? Not just bending them, but twisting them into knots. That suggests she has the power of telekinesis: being able to change the nature of things, or move objects with just the power of her mind. And I think as she was growing up, she was, either consciously or subconsciously, able to control it. Her brother said that her spoon bending was a novelty at first, a party trick to show off to their friends. But over time, the local children became scared of her, and Alice suppressed the abilities and rarely used them, just so she could fit in with her peers.

"When Anton Markos started giving her drugs, he didn't realize he was unleashing a side of her that had been buried for years. Methamphetamine removed her inhibitions and encouraged the fantasy she'd had since childhood. That she was Artemis the goddess."

He paused. "Are you still with me?"

"Yeah, I think so."

"Good. So now you have a girl, her state of mind altered by a steady intake of crystal meth, believing she's Artemis, goddess of the hunt. Images of Artemis have depicted her as the huntress, with a bow and arrow. We know that Alice used to play with toy bows when she was a child, honing her ability until she was quite proficient with it. So we have Alice now, believing she's Artemis, but instead of using a bow, she's using her mind to fire psychic arrows at her targets. That's why McBride can find no evidence to support his arrow theory. The arrows don't exist in the corporeal world, but their effects are as deadly as the real thing."

"Okay, Harry. I think I might be able to buy into that, although it's a bit of a stretch for someone who deals in cold, hard facts. Supposing you're right, it doesn't begin to explain the bear attacks. What the hell are those about?"

"Artemis again. In legend she is linked with bear cults and bear worship, and some images throughout history have depicted her as a bear. Alice embraces the Artemis myth wholeheartedly. Among other things, she is the goddess of wild animals. Perhaps she has an empathy with the beast."

"Stop!" Susan said. "I'm afraid that's a leap too far. This is where I part company with your theories. I can't accept that there's a bear wandering around loose in London and surrounding areas, controlled by Alice. Why has no one seen it, Harry? Why aren't calls of sightings lighting up the switchboard of every police station from Acton to Uxbridge? No, I don't buy it."

"Why not? Stranger things happen," Harry said flatly.

"In your world maybe. Not in mine."

"Sue, I know it's a lot to take on board, but we can't afford to ignore the possibility. Alice Logan, through no fault of her own, has become the most dangerous adversary I've ever come up against. The way she's using her powers at the moment is pretty devastating. Potentially, things could get a whole lot worse. We have to find her and find her soon, or I think many more people will die."

There was silence on the other end of the line. "Are you still there?" Harry said.

"Yes, still here. I'm just trying to digest it all. I'm wondering how we're going to find her. We've got people all over the country keeping an eye out for her, but she's managing to elude us and carry on killing, and I don't know how."

"She's hiding in plain sight. There's nothing supernatural about that. It's smoke and mirrors, the power of redirection. The Australian aborigines learned that trick generations ago, and stage illusionists are using it today. We'll find her, Sue. She can't keep this up forever."

"Did you bring everything I need?" Violet Bulmer lay propped up on pillows in her hospital bed.

Jason dropped the carrier bag onto the bed. "Do you feel up to this, Vi, considering what happened last time?"

"You're speaking, Jason, as if I have a choice. I have no choice. I have to do what I can to stop Alice. This, today, is a start."

"Will the staff here let you get away with it?"

"They don't have a choice either. Nobody's going to come in here and disturb me. I've seen to that."

Jason didn't ask how. Sometimes with Vi Bulmer you didn't want to know. He opened the bag and started planting candles on every spare flat surface of the room. He stuck two incense sticks into their brass holders, lit them and placed them on the windowsill. Then he went around the room, lighting candles.

"Do you want me to stay?" he said.

"Yes. Just sit in the chair and write down everything I might say. And I mean *everything*. Something you might find inane and boring may have a much deeper significance linked to something else. Shall we begin?"

Jason nodded, pulled out a notebook and pulled his chair up to the side of the bed.

Violet relaxed back against the pillow and closed her eyes. As her breathing deepened, she felt herself growing lighter. She let her mind drift and gradually felt it leave her body and rise up to the ceiling. It hung there for a moment, watching the room, noting how the candles burned without spluttering and how the fragrant smoke from the incense sticks swirled up towards her, filling her senses with a rich sandalwood scent, making her feel light-headed and slightly giddy. And then she allowed herself to float higher still, drifting up through the floors above, out through the roof of the hospital and away.

Jason sat there, pen poised above the pad, waiting for her to speak. After what seemed like several hours, but was perhaps only minutes, Violet's lips started moving and words issued from her mouth. *"I see trees, woodland. Tim, I can feel you."*

Jason looked to the bed. Violet lay there, her chest rising and falling as she breathed deeply. He started scribbling the words down on the pad.

"A path through the trees. A house, old, broken. A sign. Faded. Can't read it. The letters A, C, O, S. There's Alice. Cold, so cold. She can't see me. Alice, can you hear me?"

And then silence, just the steady resonance of Violet's breathing.

Chapter Thirty-Four

"Sue, it's Harry again. Can you tell me where they lost sight of Tim Logan?"

"Somewhere between Stevenage and Hitchin," Susan said. "He's riding a trail bike, and there's a lot of woodland around there. So he could be anywhere in the area. What are you thinking?"

"Nothing specific. Just trying to picture it in my mind."

"Well, if you come up with anything, call me."

Harry went up to Martin Impey's office. Martin was sitting at his desk, staring at the screen in front of him. He spun around in his seat as Harry tapped him on the shoulder.

"Can you do me a favor, Martin? I need you to call up a Hertfordshire Ordinance Survey map."

"Any particular area of Hertfordshire, Harry? It's a big county."

"Let's say from Stevenage to Letchworth and all points in between."

Martin frowned. "That's going to be at least three separate maps." He went back to his computer and started tapping keys. "Give me a minute. They'll come up on screens four, five and six."

Harry walked across to the bank of screens and waited.

"Anything specific you're looking for?"

"I'll know when I see it," Harry said, and tried to focus as the maps appeared in front of him.

Jason sat watching her, waiting for Violet Bulmer to speak again. After a few more moments her eyelids blinked open. "Damn it!" she said. "I've lost him."

"What happened?" Jason said.

"I don't know. I made a connection with him really easily. He was in this large house. An old place, derelict. I was walking through it with him, picking my way over dead leaves and debris. The floors were rotten, junk everywhere. And then we were climbing the stairs to the bedrooms. We entered one and Alice was there. She was crouching in one corner, wrapped in what looked like an old sleeping bag. She was shivering—Christ, it was cold in there. Tim spoke. 'Hello, Ally,' I think he said, and she looked up smiling, but then her eyes widened and she said, 'Aunt Vi!' And I was shunted out of Tim's mind."

"Do you think she saw you?" Jason said.

"Saw me or sensed me, or something. Jason, she's grown so powerful. It radiates out of her, a force so strong. It scared me, Jason, really scared me."

"So we're no nearer to finding Alice," Jason said.

"Oh, no. I know where she is. It's what we're going do when we find her, that's what bothers me. Can you get me Harry on the phone? I think I need to talk to him."

Harry stared at the screens, looking at trails and pathways, waiting for something to jump out at him. He started when his phone buzzed in his pocket. He took it out. "Hello, Jason. What can I do for you?"

"It's Vi, Harry—"

"How is she?" Harry said, cutting across him.

"She's been roaming again."

"How could you let her? It nearly killed her the last time."

"I couldn't stop her, Harry. You know how she gets."

"Yeah, I do."

"Anyway, she wants to talk to you."

The line went dead for a second and then Harry heard her voice.

"Vi, what the hell do you think you're playing at?"

"No lectures, Harry. I think I've found them. I went searching and managed to connect with Tim. I linked with Alice briefly the other day, when I had my coronary, but she's shut off from me now. I think she might be back on the drugs. But Tim was open. They're in a large, derelict house, somewhere close to Hitchin. I saw it, Harry. The place needs pulling down. It's standing in the middle of some woodland. Is that any help?"

"I'm standing in front of a map of that part of Hertfordshire now. It's a fairly wide search area. Do you have any more clues to guide me?"

"When Tim was approaching the house, I saw a sign for the place. It was very faded and I could barely read it, but I made out the letters *A, C, O, S*. Will that help?"

"It might, Vi. Stay on the line." He turned to Martin. "I'm looking for a house in this area." He sketched a circle on the screen. "*Roughly* this area. It's a big place and, from what Vi said, it's nearly falling down. It has the letters *A, C, O, S* in the name."

Martin returned his attention to the screen and started hitting keys again. "Jackman House," he said after a few moments. "It used to be an old folks' home ages ago. It's been empty for about twenty years—some kind of dispute as to who owns it and who's responsible for it. It's about a mile and a half south of Hitchin, in the middle of Burwell Wood."

Harry's eyes scanned the map. "Got it. Can I get a printout of this?"

"Done," Martin said, and with two keystrokes a color map chugged out of the printer.

Harry grabbed the map and took the elevator up to the next floor and McKinley's office. "Can you spare me an hour or three, John?"

"Do you want me to go on a jaunt with you again?"

"Something like that. Hertfordshire this time, leafy Hertfordshire."

"Better than an Essex industrial estate," McKinley said. "I'm in."

While McKinley was fetching his coat, Harry phoned Jason.

"Tell Vi, thanks to her, I think I've identified where they are. It's a place called Jackman House, in Burwell Wood, just outside Hitchin. John McKinley and I are going there now."

"Do you need me along? I think Vi's finished with me here."

"No, Jason. Do me a favor and stay there with Vi. John and I can handle it from here. I'll be in touch when it's over. She might need you then."

"I understand," Jason said. "You really care about her, don't you, Harry?"

"Vi and I go back a long way. She's bailed me out of some very sticky situations in the past. One time, on a particularly nasty case we were working on, she saved my life. So, yes, you could say I care about her."

"Stay safe, Harry," Jason said.

"I'm going to give it a damned good try."

"Aren't you getting your DI involved this time?" McKinley said.

Harry stared out at the London streets flashing by. "No, not this time, John. I don't think she realizes the danger Alice Logan poses. Susan knows that Alice is a threat, so if she's aware that we're going to apprehend her, Susan will call out the cavalry, and that could have disastrous consequences, especially if she enlists the help of an Armed Response team. Alice has the power to make them turn their weapons on each other, and if that doesn't work, remember the nurse at the Mayberry Clinic. Her brain was reduced to mush."

"And you think now that Alice was responsible for that?"

"I have very little doubt that it was her."

McKinley unwrapped a stick of chewing gum and popped it into his mouth. "And us? Do you think we can handle her?"

"At least we can protect ourselves against any psychic attack," Harry said. "Whether we can call a halt to her reign of terror is yet to be seen. But we're going to have a bloody good try."

Chapter Thirty-Five

As they left the London streets behind, the landscape changed around them. Rows of shops and terraced houses gave way to deep golden swathes of harvested wheat fields and lush green expanses of grazing land.

McKinley drove, chewing his gum and tapping the wheel in time to a tune playing in his head. Harry could feel the anticipation emanating from him. He was tense, as Harry was himself, at the prospect of what was to come. The likelihood of failure was very real. If he were being honest with himself, he'd put their chance of success at about fifty-fifty. So he was under no illusions about the difficulty of the task ahead of them.

They crossed the border into Hertfordshire, and Harry felt his instincts sharpening, his mind clearing of pretty much everything apart from the task in hand. "Take the next turnoff," he said.

McKinley nodded and indicated they were leaving the motorway. Soon they were driving along narrow lanes with high hedges of beech and hawthorn, and blind bends where McKinley had to reduce their speed to a cautious crawl.

Eventually Harry pointed to a lay-by in the road ahead. "Pull in there," he said. "We'll walk through the wood from here." McKinley looked around at the dense growths of alder, ash and beech, some of them dwarfed by massive oaks and horse chestnut trees.

They got out of the car and picked their way up the bank, their feet slipping on the mud left after the overnight rain. Once they reached the top of the bank, they headed north, finally locating a path overgrown by thorn-rich brambles and thick clumps of gorse. As McKinley struggled with the thorns tearing at his trouser legs, he turned back to Harry. "Why do I feel I should have dressed for the occasion? Do you know how much I paid for these shoes, for these pants? Look at them now, ruined."

"Charge them to expenses," Harry said grimly. "Not far now."

Up ahead of them, they could see where the tree growth thinned. There was a barbed-wire fence with rotting posts and rusting wire. There was a gap in the fence, a gatepost standing sentinel each side of it, what was left of the gate lying on the ground, half-covered by bindweed and thick couch grass. Affixed to one of the gateposts was a rectangular sign made from distressed plywood, the corners of the plies curled and browning. The fading black letters read *Jackman House*. In the distance they could see the house itself.

Built during the mid-Victorian Gothic period, the house had once been grand, with high, mullioned windows and a turreted roof. A few ornamental waterspouts remained, but others had fallen to the ground and lay there cracked and broken, the cast-iron gutters long rusted through and hanging from the roof.

Most of the windows had been boarded up and the doorways covered by sheets of green-painted corrugated iron.

They approached along what once had been a gravel drive, but dandelion, plantains and thistle had superseded the gravel, and there were shallow potholes in the drive, filled with brackish rainwater.

"What a dump," McKinley said as they stopped on the drive fifteen yards from the front door. "Do we go inside?"

Harry held up his hand. "Not just yet. Let's get our bearings first."

He looked to his left and right. The woodland had encroached so that it had taken over the drive. "If it was left long enough, nature would reclaim this place for itself." He looked up at the roof. Where the gutters still clung to it, buddleia had taken root, and long, arched branches of the stuff had curled down to touch the walls.

"Alice!" he called out suddenly, making McKinley start. "Alice? We know you're in there."

A few seconds passed and then Tim Logan called out. "Go away! Go away and leave us alone."

"We're here to help her, Tim. Let us help your sister. Let us help Alice."

There was no response, and they glanced up at one of the windows where the boards had been torn away. Something white flitted into and out of their view.

"Alice? Is that you? You must be cold in there. Let us take you home. You don't want to do this anymore."

"Go away," Tim yelled again. "She doesn't want to hurt you, but she will if she has to."

"Pull back to the trees," Harry said. "He means it."

The two men turned and jogged back to the cover of the trees. "So. What's plan B?" McKinley said. Harry said nothing, but stood in the shadow of a large chestnut, rubbing his chin and staring back at the house.

As they watched and tried to figure out what their next move should be, the corrugated iron sheet was pulled away from the doorway and Alice Logan stepped out into the light.

Dressed in a short white tunic, her blonde hair dirty and matted with cobwebs and twigs, the girl looked feral.

She spread her arms wide and stared at the trees. "Come, my child, come," she called.

From the right of them, Harry heard rustling as something moved through the undergrowth and trees. he and Mckinley both turned to look but all they got were impressions. A pair of red eyes looking at them from out of the shadows, glimpses of brown fur, and an undercurrent of sound made up of low growls, snapping branches and constant rustling.

Harry turned to McKinley. "Run, John, run! Back to the car!"

As they ran, the rustling became crashing, and the low growl became a deep-throated roar. McKinley glanced back and cried out as he saw a huge, dark brown bear on all fours, bounding through the bracken, gaining on him.

They found the gap in the barbed-wire fence and barreled on through, reaching the muddy bank and sliding down it to the road. They got to the car at the same time and yanked open the doors, hurling themselves inside and pulling the doors shut behind them. They looked back to the wood, but it looked calm, peaceful. The trees and undergrowth were still. Nothing moved. No bear.

It was raining, and water dripped down from the trees to splash on the woodland floor below.

"Shit!" McKinley said. "A bear. Huge."

"It's not a bear," Harry said, shaking his head.

"It looked like a bear to me," McKinley said, breathing just as heavily as Harry and sweating profusely.

"You can't just summon up bears out of thin air," Harry said.

"So if not a bear, then what?"

"A demon," Harry said. "A minor demon maybe, taking on the form of a bear, but a demon just the same. That's how it's able to move around unseen. She calls it up when she needs it. She can empathize with it, see what it sees. Experiences the kills as if she's doing them herself. But we've dealt with demons in the past, John. We can deal with this one." He stared back at the trees. "I told you she was powerful," he said thoughtfully.

"I believed you then; I believe you now. The question is what the hell are we going to do about her?"

"I'm thinking about it," Harry said.

Chapter Thirty-Six

"Ready for round two?" Harry said and pushed open the car door. He stepped out and McKinley came around the car to join him.

"So, what's the plan?" he said.

"I haven't got one," Harry said. "We're just going to have to play this by ear."

"I was worried you were going to say that."

"Just stay vigilant," Harry said. "Remember, it's not a bear. We can defeat it."

Together they made their way back into the wood.

The rain was starting to lash down, the full force of it deflected by the branches overhead, but they were soaked within minutes. They reached the fence and passed through the gate, finding themselves again on the weed-strewn drive.

They stood there on the gravel, staring up at the house, their gazes searching the building, looking for any sign of Alice or Tim. They heard a noise behind them, something crunching over the gravel. Harry turned to see Violet Bulmer, in a wheelchair, emerging from the trees, being pushed towards them by Jason West. They stopped a yard behind them.

"Vi?" Harry said, but she put a finger to her lips to hush him.

"This started with me," she said, her voice strong, like iron. "It will end with me. Now stand back. All of you."

She put her hands on the arms of the chair and pushed herself upright. She stood there as the rain poured down, flattening her copper-gray hair to her head.

"Alice! Tim! Show yourselves, this instant."

The three men held back as gradually the undergrowth behind them began to rustle. All three turned to face the trees.

The bear broke from the undergrowth and started loping towards them, savage teeth bared, a growl rising in volume to a baritone roar. Each of the three men raised their hands in front of them and made passes through the air.

When it was within twelve feet of them, the bear stopped running and reared up on its hind legs, the roar becoming deafening. McKinley made another pass with his hands, air-drawing the sign of a pentagram, and then stabbed his hand forward, index finger pointing. The bear staggered and dropped back to all fours, shaking its huge, shaggy head as if stunned.

As the rain continued to fall, it appeared to be washing the dark brown fur from the creature's body. The fur slipped from its haunches, dripping to the ground like brown sludge, leaving behind grayish, dirty pink, translucent skin, threaded with blue veins and pulsating red arteries. The head was the last thing to be denuded of fur. The eyes turned from red to dull gray, and the mouth opened once more to roar but could only manage a watery croak.

The head had shrunk to little more than a misshapen skull covered by thin gray skin. The demon lifted a sinewy arm and held it out as if to ward off a blow, as Harry and Jason, following McKinley's lead, moved the air in front of them and sent another wave of energy at the demon. It stood there for a few more seconds, until the skin along the length of its spine split open and the flesh began to slough off its bones.

Finally, it collapsed, falling to one side, where it lay as the pounding rain slowly dissolved it, turning the body into nothing more than a muddy pool that soaked into the gravel drive.

They looked to the woods but nothing moved, nothing came rushing towards them, and all they could see were the trees.

"It's over, Alice," Violet called out. "Show yourself. Come out into the light and finish this now."

Silence settled over the house and woodland, broken only by the sound of the rain splashing on the drive and lashing the walls of the house.

As they watched, the corrugated iron sheet was still pulled to one side and Alice Logan stepped through the doorway and stood there on the porch, the diaphanous material of her short robe soaking up the rain, becoming transparent. Tim hovered in the doorway behind her, whey-faced, his whole body trembling.

"Let's end this, Alice," Violet said steadily.

"Not Alice. I'm *Artemis*," the girl said in a strong, commanding voice.

As Alice stood there in the rain, she raised her left arm, her fist aiming at Violet. Violet crossed her arms in front of her chest. Slowly Alice brought her other arm up behind her, arched, taut as if drawing on a bowstring.

Tim seemed to come from nowhere. He dashed from the doorway and stood, putting his body between Alice and Violet. "No. Ally! This has to stop!"

The girl stared as if challenging him, and then her fingers twitched and Tim cried out, staggering backwards as a red hole appeared in his forehead and the back of his skull blew outwards. His legs folded under him and he crumpled to the ground.

Alice stared at his twisted, fallen body dispassionately. "You did this," she hissed at Violet, and then raised her arm again, cocking her head to the left, taking aim.

She drew her arm back behind her, but as the fingers of her right hand splayed, Violet threw her arms open wide. There was the sound of something whistling through the air, followed by a dull thud.

Alice looked down at the crimson stain blossoming on the front of her dress, and then she looked at Violet with a surprised expression on her face.

Vi stared back at her steadily, but the tears were already falling down her cheeks.

Alice's mouth opened in a small *O* and she toppled backwards, hitting the ground, her dead eyes staring at the rain as if looking searchingly up to the heavens.

Violet turned away and started to walk back to the three men.

"Are you okay?" Harry said.

Violet nodded, took another step and then threw her hands to her head and cried out.

"You killed my baby!'

Harry turned in the direction of the voice. Through the rain, he saw Stephanie

Logan walking out from the trees. Hair plastered flat to her head, her eyes wild, she approached Alice's fallen body. Tears were pouring from her eyes, mingling with the rain spattering her cheeks

Violet was still clutching her head.

Stephanie crouched down beside Alice and gently closed her eyes. "Sleep now," she said, and then got to her feet, turned to face Violet and raised her hand. Violet cried out and staggered backwards,

"You knew she was here, Stephanie," Harry said. "You knew all along."

Stephanie looked at him, contempt on her face. "Of course I knew," she said.

"But why did you say nothing?"

"My beloved Artemis…I loved her so much. We were happy once…until that bastard…that scum, Strasser, came into her life and took her away from me."

"You encouraged the fantasy," Harry said. "You bought the books, made Alice believe she was Artemis."

"*She was Artemis!*" Stephanie screamed at him. "She was always special."

"You used me," Violet said. "Used me to bring Alice back to you."

Stephanie spun towards her, venom in her eyes, raised her hand again, and Violet screamed.

"Yes, sister, I used you. I knew you'd find her. Because you're the one with the power, aren't you? You're the one Mother would praise and lavish all her attention on, because you had your *gifts*, the powers that made you so much like her. But what about me? I was special too, but she never saw me, because your shadow was too long and I could never get out from under it."

"I had no idea—" Violet started, but Stephanie's brow creased, and something flashed in her expression Violet reeled backwards as if struck.

"Well, now you know, Violet. I have powers. I've always had powers, greater than yours. When Alice was born, I swore then that she would never grow up in anyone's shadow as I had done. Yes, I helped her realize the greatness she was destined for. I fed her imagination, helped her take control of the gifts that had been passed down to her, because *my* blood was flowing through her veins."

"You created a monster," Harry said.

"No, Mr. Bailey. I created a *goddess. I created Artemis!*" Stephanie said coldly.

She raised her arm again, but before she could deliver another psychic jolt, both Jason and McKinley stepped forward, hands raised to create a psychic barrier that enveloped Harry and Violet.

Stephanie staggered backwards.

Violet looked up at her sister bleakly. "You must really hate me," she said.

Stephanie laughed harshly. "I've despised you since we were children. Always playing second fiddle, always second best. But I did something you can only dream about. I became a mother... and *I gave birth to a goddess.*"

"And you've lived your sad, pathetic life through your daughter," Violet said. "And in living your life, you destroyed your precious daughter and, in turn, your son. I feel sorry for you, Stephanie. I really do."

"And now I will destroy you and the lives of the pathetic people who care about you." Stephanie stretched her arms wide, and her eyes rolled back in her head. Thunder crashed overhead and the rain came down in torrents, the wind gusting, whipping the rain into a maelstrom that knocked Jason and McKinley off their feet and sent them sprawling into the mud.

Harry grabbed Violet's hand. "Together!" he yelled at her over the noise of the storm and gripped her hand tightly.

And they were one. One entity, one mind emitting wave after wave of psychic energy.

For an instant Stephanie was lifted from the ground, rising ten feet into the air. From the center of the vortex she screamed, a thin, piercing wail that rose above the noise of the tumult, to be sucked away in the gale. And as abruptly as it had started, the storm died, and she fell to the ground, landing in a crumpled heap at their feet, her head lying at an impossible angle, neck broken.

"Vi, I..." Harry said.

She shook her head. "Not now, Harry. Not now."

"How's Vi doing?" Susan said.

Harry shifted in the bed and took his cup of tea from the bedside cabinet. "The last I heard, she's doing okay. Jason's moved into her house in Chelsea. She's given him three rooms upstairs to convert into his own flat. Although she won't admit it, she needs someone in her life. She lost her family."

"Has she spoken about what happened that day?"

"Not to me, and I doubt that she ever will. She's in mourning, and will be for many years to come." He sipped his tea and changed the subject. "So what are you going to do, now you've quit the force?"

"Take a holiday, I suppose. I haven't had one in ten years."

"Where do you fancy?"

"Somewhere hot. Not Greece," she said firmly. "Definitely not Greece. The Algarve perhaps. Maybe I'll go out there and search for locations where I can open a bar."

"Sounds good," Harry said.

"I heard they had problems out there finding bar staff who won't drink the profits. Got any suggestions?"

Harry put his cup down again and took her in his arms. "I might be able to come up with a name," he said, and kissed her. "I just might."

About the Author

Len Maynard & Mick Sims are the authors of several thriller novels, including *Nightmare City, Stronghold,* and *Stillwater,* and the Department 18 books *The Eighth Witch* and *A Plague Of Echoes,* all from Samhain. *Mother Of Demons* is Department 18 book 5. *Convalescence,* an e-novella, is scheduled in 2015.

They are currently working on more thrillers. They have been published in romance under a pseudonym, have had nine story collections published, and are currently completing the tenth. They have had numerous stories published in a variety of anthologies and magazines. They have won awards with their screenplays. They also work as editors, and do ghost writing projects, and have been essayists, reviewers and small press publishers.

www.maynard-sims.com

A modern ghost story

Stillwater
© 2015 Maynard Sims

Life was good for Beth, once. Now a car crash has left her confined to a wheelchair. To help her recuperate and rebuild her life, she's leased Stillwater, a house with a lake in the countryside. But her dreams of peace and quiet are thwarted when she realizes she's not alone. A girl who once lived at Stillwater—until she drowned in the lake—has never left, and she does not seem pleased by Beth's presence. Beth sets out to solve the mystery of Stillwater. But can she find a strength she doesn't know she possesses as she fights the fury of the dead girl, and tries to establish herself as the true mistress and keeper of the Stillwater house and lake?

Enjoy the following excerpt for Stillwater:

The dinner, when it finally arrived, was superb. Gwen was a great cook. The meat fell away from the bone as soon as the knife touched it, and the carrots and broccoli were crisp and tasted fresh, unlike vegetables Beth had bought in the past from supermarkets.

"You can thank Arthur for those," Gwen said, when Beth commented on them. "He's been blessed with green fingers. Our garden is like an allotment."

Sitting opposite Arthur Latham Beth watched his face flush with embarrassment, and not a little pride. The pair of them seemed well suited to each other. Beth felt a twinge of envy.

"Tell me," Beth said. "Have you ever met the owner of my house?"

"Bernard Franklin? No, I've never seen him," Gwen said. "Arthur has though."

"Only very briefly," Latham said. "I saw him around town from time to time, and bumped into him once or twice at the post office. I tried to make conversation with him, but he didn't want to know. I thought he was a surly devil."

"Really?" Beth said. "Why was that?"

"Well, this is a fairly friendly community. I wouldn't say we're in each other's pockets, but we all pass the time of day, and if push comes to shove we all look out for each other. Franklin on the other hand wouldn't have anything to do with us; kept very much to himself. And his daughter wasn't much better. Jessica, her name was. She'd walk around the village with her nose in the air, and wouldn't really talk to anyone, not even the people her own age. I don't think she was deliberately rude. Mr. Samuels who runs the grocer's told me she was always very pleasant to him. I put it down to the way she'd been brought up. Thought we were too normal, too boring."

"It was very sad what happened to her," Gwen said.

"What was that?" Beth asked.

"She died…drowned…a few days after her seventeenth birthday."

"How did it happen?"

"An accident," Latham said. "So the inquest found. She'd gone for a swim in the lake, and got entangled in some weeds. At least, that was the theory."

"You sound skeptical," Beth said.

"I was then. I am now," Latham said. "She was a pupil at Greysmeade, the local high school, for the short time she was living here. I was a teacher there before I retired, and I remember that Jessica Franklin was in the school swimming team. She wasn't a popular member but they tolerated her because she was such a strong swimmer. She helped the school bring home a number of county trophies. It seemed unlikely to me a girl like that would have become victim to some pondweed."

"Did you give evidence at the inquest?" Beth asked.

"Oh yes, I gave my opinion, but it didn't count for much. The postmortem also found a high level of alcohol in Jessica's blood. Given those details the verdict was a foregone conclusion. Poor girl."

"That's very sad," Beth said.

"I think it broke her father. From what I could tell he doted on his daughter once his wife left him. I think that when Jessica died it finished him. He moved away…abroad…Malta, I think…but kept the house on. He returned to England after a while, but settled near Cambridge. He never came back to live at Stillwater, and it's been a rental property ever since."

"How long ago did all this happen?"

"About fifteen years now," Gwen Latham said.

"And the house has been let out ever since?"

"Yes, but only sporadically," Latham said. "You're the first tenant in about four years. The place was standing empty before you came along. I must say, it was a relief to many of us in the village when we heard that Stillwater was going to be occupied again."

"Why's that?"

"What is it they say?" Latham said. "Nature abhors a vacuum? Just six months ago you wouldn't have recognized the place. The garden was completely overgrown. The rhododendrons were rampant, and so many plants had been strangled by the bindweed."

"The house was in a shocking state of disrepair. Houses die if they're not occupied, and Stillwater was well on the way." Gwen continued. "Many of the windows were broken and at least three of the shutters had gone. The gutters were down, and the paths were cracked and broken. It was a vandals' paradise." She paused, noticing the look of surprise on Beth's face. "Oh yes, even here in the back of beyond we still fall foul of many of society's ills. Luckily Falmer's are a fairly conscientious company. They put the place straight. I think the only part of the estate that wasn't refurbished was the lake. No one touched that."

"Which is just as well," Latham said. "Considering that Jessica met her end there. In my opinion, to tart it up would, I don't know…tarnish her memory."

Gwen Latham laughed sharply. "You sentimental old fool," she said tartly, and then, to Beth, "You listen to him and you'd think the whole village was in mourning for her."

"And that wasn't the case?"

"Well, I didn't shed any tears for her, and I can think of many who shared my view of her. Good riddance, I said at the time."

"Gwen!" Latham said. "That's not very charitable."

"Maybe, but I still think the girl was a troublemaker."

"You've no evidence for that. Just local gossip."

"Well, as they say, there's no smoke…"

"Enough!" Latham said. He turned to Beth. "What must you think of us, Beth? Honestly, we're not small-minded people. Would you like a coffee?"

"I'd love one, but decaf if you have it, otherwise I'll spend the night bouncing off the walls."

"No problem," Latham said, and left the room.

Beth glanced across at Gwen, who was grinning mischievously. She caught Beth's questioning look.

"Oh, take no notice of us. Arthur's a lovely man and I care for him deeply. He just has blind spots in certain areas. He's far too trusting. He tries to see the good in everyone. But sometimes there's no good to be found."

"And that applied to Jessica Franklin?"

"In my opinion, and that of many others in the village."

SAMHAIN
P U B L I S H I N G

It's all about the story...

Romance

HORROR

www.samhainpublishing.com